BIG PLANET

COLLECTORS' EDITION
SF
GOLLANCZ · GOLLANCZ

Also by Jack Vance
in Millennium

Emphyrio
Tales of the Dying Earth

BIG
PLANET

Jack Vance

VICTOR GOLLANCZ
LONDON

An abridged version of this novel was published in 1957 by
Avalon Books and subsequently reprinted. This edition follows the first
unabridged version in book form.

This edition published in Great Britain in 2000 by
Victor Gollancz
An imprint of Orion Books Ltd
Orion House, 5 Upper St Martin's Lane, London WC2H 9EA

Second impression published in Great Britain in 2002
by Gollancz
An imprint of the Orion Publishing Group

Distributed in the United States of America
by Sterling Publishing Co, Inc
387 Park Avenue South,
New York NY 10016-8810.

A CIP catalogue record for this book is available
from the British Library

ISBN 0 57507 117 6

Printed in Great Britain by
The Guernsey Press Co. Ltd, Guernsey, C.I.

BIG
PLANET

Contents

1

Sabotage

Arthur Hidders, he called himself. He wore Earth-style clothes, and, except for the length of his hair and his mustache rings, he looked the complete Earthman—which, in a sense, he was. His age was indeterminate; the exact panel of races which had gone into his make-up was a secret six hundred years gone. He stood an easy five foot six; he was light, with delicate features centered rather too closely in a large round head, which obviously held many brains.

Turning away from the porthole out on space, he fixed old Pianza with a gaze of almost child-like ingenuousness. "That's all very interesting—but doesn't it seem, well, futile?"

"Futile?" Pianza said with great dignity. "I'm afraid I don't understand you."

Hidders made a careless gesture, taking few pains to hide his opinion of Pianza: a well-meaning man, perhaps a trifle dense. "Earth-Central has sent commissions to Big Planet once a generation for the last five hundred years. Sometimes the commission returns alive, more often not. In either case nothing is accomplished. A few investigators lose their lives, much money is spent, Big Planet tempers—forgive me—are ruffled, and things go on, regrettably, as before."

Pianza, certainly well-meaning, not at all dense, reflected that Hidders' air of naivete comported poorly with his professed occupation of fur-trading. Also, thought Pianza, how could a Big Planet fur-trader—a naive fur-trader—accumulate the exchange necessary to buy passage to Earth? He answered gravely. "What you say is true, but this time perhaps events will turn out differently."

Hidders raised his eyebrows, spread out his hands. "Has Big Planet changed? Has Earth-Central changed?"

Pianza looked uneasily around the lounge—empty except for the nun who sat statue-quiet, the visible section of her thin white face rapt in meditation. Big Planet lay close ahead; the Bajarnum of Beaujolais could not possibly know of their approach. Pianza committed an indiscretion.

"Conditions are different," he admitted. "A great deal different. The former commissions were sent out to—well, let us say, to soothe Earth consciences. We knew there was murder, torture, terror on Big Planet; we knew something had to be done." He smiled sadly. "The easiest gesture was to send out commissions. The commissions invariably made the same report: nothing could be done that was not being done already at the Enclave—unless Earth-Central wanted to expand, to take full responsibility for Big Planet."

"Interesting," said Hidders. "You have the gift of expressing complicated ideas in simple language. And now?"

Pianza eyed him doubtfully. The butter had become a little thick. "Now there's something new on Big Planet: the Bajarnum of Beaujolais."

"Yes, yes—I've frequently traveled through his realms."

"Well, on Big Planet there are probably hundreds of rulers no less cruel, arrogant, arbitrary—but the Bajarnum, as you certainly must be aware, is expanding his empire, his range of activities, and not only on Big Planet but elsewhere."

"Ah," said Hidders. "So you come to investigate Charley Lysidder, Bajarnum of Beaujolais."

"Yes," muttered Pianza. "You might say so. And this time we have the authority to act."

"If he learns of your plans, he will no doubt react with rancor and violence."

"We realize that," stammered Pianza, wishing now that he could disavow the conversation. "But I'm sure he won't learn until we're ready."

"Perhaps you're right," said Hidders gravely. "Let us hope so."

A dark-skinned man of medium height came into the lounge. His muscles lay close under his skin; he moved quickly, with sharp definite motions. This was Claude Glystra, Executive Chairman of the commission.

Glystra looked swiftly around the lounge, ice-colored glances, hard, searching, just short of suspicious. He joined Hidders and Pianza at the porthole, pointed to a flaming yellow sun close ahead. "There's Phaedra, we'll be on Big Planet in a few hours."

A gong rang. "Lunch," said Pianza, rising with a feeling of relief. The purpose of the commission was hardly a secret to anyone aboard the ship; however, he had been uncomfortably explicit in his talk with Hidders. He was glad to push the whole matter to the back of his mind.

Glystra led the way from the saloon, pausing at the

9

door to let the nun sweep ahead in a billow of black vestments.

"Peculiar creature," muttered Pianza.

Glystra laughed. "There's no one on Big Planet but peculiar people; that's why they're there. If she wants to convert them to her own private peculiarity, that's her privilege."

Hidders nodded with lively emphasis. "Perfect democracy on Big Planet, eh Mr Glystra?"

Pianza watched expectantly; Glystra was nothing if not outspoken. Glystra did not fail him.

"Perfect anarchy, Mr Hidders."

In silence they descended the spiral to the dining saloon, took their places. One by one the other members of the commission entered. First was Cloyville, big, booming, florid; then Ketch, dark, drawn and saturnine, like the "Before" in a laxative advertisement. Next came Bishop, the youngest man on the commission, sheep-faced and seal-smooth, with a brain full of erudition and a tendency toward hypochondria. He satisfied the one with a portable microfilm library, the other with a portable medicine-chest. Behind him, and last, was Darrot, erect and military with carrot-colored hair, lips compressed as if against an imminent outburst of temper.

The meal was placid, but over-hung with a sense of excitement, almost tension, which persisted, grew stronger all afternoon as the bulk of Big Planet spread across the field of vision. Horizons belled out, blotted Phaedra from the sky, and the space-ship settled into the darkness.

There was a shock, a lurch, a perceptible change of direction. Glystra spun away from the window. The lights flickered, died, then glowed weakly. Glystra ran up the spiral toward the bridge. At the top landing stood a squat man in ship's uniform—Abbigens, the radio operator and purser. Lank blond hair hung down his forehead. He watched Glystra's approach with narrow eyes set far apart.

"What's the trouble?" Glystra demanded sharply. "What's going on?"

"Don't know, Mr Glystra. I tried to get in myself; I found the door locked."

"The ship feels out of control, as if we're going to crash!"

"Don't worry your head about that, Mr Glystra. We've got emergency landing gear to set us down—automatic stuff. There may be a bit of a thump, but if we sit quiet in the saloon we're safe enough."

Gently he took Glystra's arm. Glystra shook him off, returned to the door. Solid as a section of the wall.

He ran back down the steps, railing at himself for not taking precautions against just such a chance. To land anywhere on Big Planet except Earth Enclave meant tragedy, debacle, cataclysm. He stood in the saloon doorway; there was a babble of voices, white faces turned to him. Cloyville, Darrot, Pianza, Bishop, Ketch, Hidders and the nun. All there. He ran to the engine room; the door opened under his hands. Corbus, the easygoing chief engineer, pushed him back.

"We've got to get to the life-boats," barked Glystra.

"No more life-boats.'

"*No more life-boats!* What's happened to them?" Glystra demanded.

"They've been ejected. It's stick by the ship, there's nothing else to do."

"But the captain, the mate—"

"They don't answer the telephone."

11

"But what on Earth happened?"

Corbus' reply was drowned by a siren which filled the air, already made mad by the flickering light, with clangor.

Abbigens came into the saloon. He looked around with an air of triumph, nodded toward someone. Who? Glystra twisted his head. Too late. White faces, open mouths. And now—a picture he would never forget: the door swung open, the mate staggered in, his hand held as if he were rubbing his throat. His face was the colour of raw potato; ghastly dark ribbons striped the front of his jumper. He pointed a terrible trembling finger at Abbigens. Blood rasped in his lungs, his knees folded, he fell to the deck. His hand slipped to show a second mouth under his chin.

Glystra stared at the squat man with the blond hair falling thickly down his forehead.

Dark shadows rushed up past the saloon ports. A monstrous splintered instant: the floor of the saloon struck up. The lights went out; there was a hoarse crying.

Glystra crawled up the floor. He sensed walls toppling; he saw a sudden dark motion, heard jarring thunder, and then felt an instant of pain. . . .

Glystra rose toward consciousness like a waterlogged timber. He opened his eyes; vision reached his brain.

He lay on a low bed at the rear of a plank-walled cottage. With a feverish movement he half-raised on the cot, propped himself on an elbow, stared out the open door, and it seemed that he was seeing the most wonderful sight of his life.

He looked out on a green slope, spangled with yellow and red flowers, which rose to a forest. The gables of a village showed through the foliage, quaint gables of carved dark-brown timber. The entire landscape was drenched in a tingling golden-white radiance; every color shone with jewel-like clarity.

Three girls in peasant dress moved across the field of his vision; they were dancing a merry jig which flung their belled blue and red skirts back and forth, side to side. Glystra could hear music, the drone of a concertina, tinkle of mandolin and guitar.

He slumped back to the cot, closed his eyes. A picture from the golden ages. A beautiful dream.

The thud of footsteps roused him. Watching under half-cracked eyelids he saw Pianza and Cloyville enter the cottage: the one tidy, gray, quiet; the other puffing, red-faced, effusive. Behind came a fresh-faced girl with blonde pigtails, carrying a tray.

Glystra struggled up on his elbows again. Pianza said soothingly, "Relax, Claude. You're a sick man."

Glystra demanded, "Was anyone killed?" He was surprised to find his voice so weak.

There was a moment's silence.

"Well? Who got it?"

"The stewards. They had gone to hide in the shell. And the nun. Apparently she went into her cabin just before the crash. It's twenty feet underground now. Of course the captain and the mate, both with their throats cut."

Glystra closed his eyes. "How long has it been?"

"About four days."

He lay passive a few seconds, thinking. "What's been happening?"

"The ship's a total loss," said Cloyville. He pulled out a chair, seated himself. "Broken in three pieces. A wonder any of us came out alive."

The girl laid the tray on the bed, knelt, prepared to feed Glystra with a horn spoon.

Glystra looked up ruefully. "Is this what's been going on?"

"You had to be taken care of," said Pianza. He patted the girl's head. "This is Natilien-Thilssa. Nancy for short. She's an excellent nurse."

Cloyville winked slyly. "Lucky dog."

Glystra moved back from the spoon. "I can feed myself," he said shortly. He looked up at Pianza. "Where are we?"

Pianza frowned slightly, as if he had hoped to avoid serious discussion. "The village of Jubilith—somewhere near the northeastern tip of Beaujolais."

Glystra pressed his lips together. "It could hardly be worse. Naturally they planned to drop us closer to Grosgarth, right into the Bajarnum's lap." He struggled up on his elbow. "I'm astonished we haven't been taken up already."

Pianza looked out the door. "We're rather isolated, and naturally there are no communications . . . We've been nervous, I'll admit."

The last terrible scene in the saloon rose before Glystra's mind. "Where's Abbigens?"

"Abbigens? Oh, he's gone. Disappeared."

Glystra groaned under his breath. Pianza looked uneasily at Cloyville, who frowned.

"Why didn't you kill him?" Glystra moaned.

All Pianza could do was shake his head. Cloyville said, "He got away."

"There was someone else too," said Glystra weakly.

Pianza leaned forward, his eyes sharp and gray. "Someone else? Who?"

14

"I don't know. Abbigens slaughtered the captain and the mate, the other sabotaged the motors, discharged the life-boats." He heaved restlessly on the couch. The girl put a cool hand on his forehead. "I've been unconscious four days. Extraordinary."

"You've been sedated," said Pianza, "to keep you resting. For a while you were out of your head, climbing out of bed, fighting, yelling."

2

Forty-thousand-mile Trek

Glystra sat up against Nancy's restraining hand, felt the base of his skull. He tried to rise to his feet. Cloyville jumped up. 'For Heaven's sake, Claude, take it easy," he admonished.

Glystra shook his head. "We've got to get out of here. Fast. Think. Where's Abbigens? He's gone to report to Charley Lysidder, the Bajarnum." He stood swaying. Nancy came to cajole him back to the cot, but instead, leaning on her shoulder, he went to the door and stood in the wash of golden-white sunlight, the Big Planet panorama before him. Pianza brought a chair, Glystra sank into it.

The cottage, the forest, the village were situated halfway up the face of a slope, vast beyond Earthly conception. Above, Glystra could see no sharp termination or ridge; the land melted into pale blue distance. Below was a vista so grand and airy that after the first few miles the eye could sense only the spread of territory, meadows and forests becoming a green, blue, beige blur.

Cloyville stretched his heavy arms out into the warmth. "Here's where I'm coming in my old age." He yawned. "We never should have wasted Big Planet on the freaks."

Nancy slipped into the house with a stiff back.

Cloyville chuckled. "I guess she thought I was calling her a freak."

"You'll never have an old age," said Glystra, "if we don't clear out of here." He looked up and down the slope. "Where's the ship?"

"Up in the forest a little bit."

"And how far are we from Beaujolais?"

Cloyville looked southwest diagonally up the slope. "The borders of Beaujolais are vague. Over the top of the slope is a deep valley, apparently volcanic. Full of hot springs, fumaroles, geysers, so they tell me—the valley of the Glass-Blowers. Last year the Bajarnum moved in with his troops, and now the valley is part of Beaujolais. To date he hasn't sent officials or tax-collectors to Jubilith, but they're expected every day, together with a garrison."

"Why a garrison? To keep order?"

Cloyville gestured down the slope. "Protection against the nomads—gypsies, they call 'em."

"Mmmph." Glystra looked up at the village. "They don't seem to have suffered too much ... How far is Grosgarth?"

"As near as I can make it, two hundred miles south. There's a garrison town—Montmarchy, they call it—about fifty miles southeast along the slope."

"Fifty miles." Glystra considered. "That's probably where Abbigens headed for. . . ." A heavy metallic crash sounded from the forest. Glystra looked questioningly at Pianza.

"They're cutting up the ship. It's the most metal they've seen in their lives. We've made them all millionaires."

"Until the Bajarnum confiscates the whole thing," said Cloyville.

"We've got to get out," Glystra muttered, twisting in

his chair. "We've got to get to the Enclave—somehow. . . ."

Pianza pursed his lips doubtfully. "It's around the planet, forty thousand miles."

Glystra struggled up to his feet. "We've got to get out of here. We're sitting ducks. If we're caught, it's our lives. Charley Lysidder will make an example of us. . . .Where's the rest of the ship's company?"

Pianza nodded toward the village. "We've been given a big house. Hidders has gone."

"Gone? Where to?"

"Grosgarth." He added hastily, "He says he'll take a barge to Marwan Gulf and join one of the beach caravans to Wale."

"Hmmm. The stewards dead, the captain and mate dead, the nun dead, Abbigens gone, Hidders gone—" he counted on his fingers "—that leaves eight. The commission and two engine room officers. You'd better bring them all down here and we'll have a council of war."

Eyes troubled, Glystra watched Pianza and Cloyville climbing to the village, then turned his attention down the slope. Beaujolain soldiers approaching during the daylight would be visible for many miles. Glystra gave thanks for the non-metallic crust of Big Planet. No metal, no machinery, no electricity, no long distance communication.

Nancy appeared from the cottage. She had changed her puffed blue skirt for a parti-colored coverall, a harlequin suit of red and orange motley. Over her hair she wore a close fitting cap, set with two-inch spines of hair waxed to golden points.

18

Glystra stared a moment. Nancy whirled before him, pirouetted on one toe, with the other leg bent at the knee.

Glystra said, "Are all the girls at Jubilith as lovely as you are?"

She smiled, tilted her face to the sun. "I'm not from Jubilith . . . I'm an outlander."

"So? From where?"

She gestured to the north. "From Veillevaux Forest. My father had the gift, and for many miles people came to ask the future—even some who might have made the pilgrimage to Myrtlesee Fountain."

"Myrtlesee Fountain?" Glystra opened his mouth to inquire, then reflected that any explanation would be couched in the intricacies of a strange culture, and closed his mouth. Best to listen, to observe, let knowledge come in manageable doses.

"My father grew rich," continued Nancy. "He trained me in the crafts. I travelled to Grosgarth and Calliope and Wale and through the Stemvelt Canals, and I went outland as a troubadour, with fine companies, and we saw many towns and castles and beautiful sights." She shuddered. "And evil also. Much evil, at Glaythree . . ." Tears welled into her eyes, her shoulders sagged. She said forlornly, "When I returned to Veillevaux Forest I found ruin and desolation. The gypsies from North Heath had raided the village and burnt the house of my father with all my family inside. And I wandered here to Jubilith to learn to dance, that I might dance away my grief. . . ."

Glystra studied her closely. Marvelous mobility of feature—sparkle of eye, lilt of voice when she spoke of joy— a mouth that was never quite in repose. And when she dwelt on her grief her eyes became large and wistful, and the nervous beauty of her face and body seemed to become less explicit, glowing from some wonderful region inside her mind, as light shines from the inner part of a star.

"And how is it that you were selected to nurse me?"

She shrugged, studied the backs of her hands. "I'm an outlander; I know the methods of Grosgarth—some of which have been learned from Earth books. *Naisuka*."

Glystra looked up in puzzlement, repeated the word. "What is that?"

"It's a Beajolais word." She settled herself to the ground at his feet, leaned back against the wall, stretched with the easy looseness of a kitten. "It means—well, it's what makes a person decide to do things for no reason whatever."

He pointed down the slope. "What country is that nestled down there?"

She turned half on her side, propped herself on one elbow. "The Jubilith claiming ends at the Tsalombar Woods." She indicated a far line of forest. "The Tree-people live there, above the tritchsod."

Another idiom unfamiliar to Glystra.

Up by the village the Earthmen appeared. Glystra watched their approach. Guilt in any one of them seemed as remote as guilt in Nancy. But someone had helped Abbigens, someone had burnt out the motors. Of course it might have been Arthur Hidders, and he was gone.

"Sit down," said Glystra. They took seats on the turf. Glystra looked doubtfully at Nancy. She smiled up cheerfully, made no move to rise; indeed, settled herself more comfortably, stretching her legs, pointing her toes—exotic as a rare bird.

Glystra hesitated, then turned back to the men. "We're

in a tough spot, although I suppose I don't need to belabor the point."

No one spoke.

"We're shipwrecked with no possibility of getting help from Earth. As far as technical superiority goes, we're no better off than the people of the village. Maybe worse. They understand their tools, their materials; we don't. If we had unlimited time, we might be able to patch up some kind of radio and call the Enclave. We don't have that time. Any minute we can expect soldiers to take us to Grosgarth. . . . In Grosgarth the Bajarnum will make an example of us. He doesn't want interference, he'll make sure we're aware of it. We've got one chance, that's to get out of Beaujolais, put miles behind us."

He paused, looked from face to face. Pianza was mild, non-committal, Cloyville's big forehead was creased in a heavy frown, Ketch was petulantly digging at the ground with a bit of sharp gravel. Bishop's face was faintly troubled, with little puckers like inverted V's over his eyes. Darrot ran a hand through his sparse red hair, muttered something to Ketch, who nodded. Corbus the chief engineer sat quietly, as if unconcerned. Vallusser the second engineer glared, as if Glystra were the cause of his difficulties. He said in a thick voice, "What happens when we escape. Where do we escape to? There's nothing out there—" he waved his hand down the slope "—but wild men. They'll kill us. Some of them are cannibals."

Glystra shrugged. "You're free to do whatever you like, save your skin the best way you can. Personally I see one way out. It's hard, it's long, it's dangerous. Maybe it's impossible. It's close to certain not all of us will make it. But we want to escape with our lives, we want to go home. That means—" he accented his words heavily "—one

21

place on Big Planet. The Enclave. We've got to get to the Enclave."

"Sounds good," said Cloyville. "I'm all for it. How do we do it?"

Glystra grinned. "The only means of locomotion we've got—our feet."

"Feet?" Cloyville's voice rose.

"Sounds like a pretty stiff hike," said Darrot.

Glystra shrugged. "There's no use fooling ourselves. We've got one chance to get back to Earth—that's make Earth Enclave. The only way to get there is to start."

'But forty thousand miles?' Cloyville protested plaintively. 'I'm a big man, hard on my feet.'

'We'll pick up pack-animals,' said Glystra. 'Buy them, steal them, we'll get them somehow.'

"But forty thousand miles," muttered Cloyville.

Glystra nodded. "It's a long way. But if we find the right kind of river, we'll float. Or maybe, find a ship, sail around the coast."

"Can't be done," said Bishop. "The Australian Peninsula reaches down, curves back east. We'd have to wait till we reached Henderland, then cut down, around the Blackstone Cordillera, to the Parmarbo. And, according to the Big Planet Almanac, the Parmarbo is virtually unnavigable due to reefs, pirates, carnivorous sea anemones and weekly hurricanes."

Cloyville groaned again. Glystra heard a sound from Nancy, and looked down, saw her mouth quivering in efforts to restrain a giggle. He rose to his feet, and Pianza watched him doubtfully. "How do you feel, Claude?"

"I'm weak. But tomorrow I'll be as good as new. Nothing wrong with me a little exercise won't cure. One thing we can be thankful for—"

"What's that?" asked Cloyville.

Glystra motioned to his feet. "Good boots. Water-proof, wear-proof. We'll need them."

Cloyville ruefully inspected his big torso. "I suppose the paunch will work off."

Glystra glanced around the circle. "Any other ideas? You, Vallusser?"

Vallusser shook his head. "I'll stay with the crowd."

"Good. Now here's the program. We've got to make up packs. We want all the metal we can conveniently carry; it's precious on Big Planet. Each of us ought to be able to manage fifteen pounds. Tools and knives would be best, but I suppose we'll have to take what we can salvage . . . Then we'll want clothes, a change apiece. Ship's chart of Big Planet, if available. A compass. Everyone had better find himself a good knife, a blanket, and most important— handweapons. Has anyone checked the ship?"

Corbus put his hand in his blouse, displayed the black barrel of an ion-discharge pistol. "This belonged to the Captain. I helped myself."

"I've got my two," said Cloyville.

"There should be one in my cabin aboard ship," said Pianza. "There was no way in yesterday, but maybe I can squeeze in somehow."

"There's another in mine," said Glystra. He put his hands on the arm of the chair, rose to his feet. "We'd better get started."

"You'd better rest," said Darrot gruffly. "You'll need all your strength. I'll see that your pack is made up."

Glystra relaxed without embarrassment. "Thanks. Maybe we'll make better time."

*

23

The seven men filed uphill, into the forest of silky blue-green trees. Glystra watched them from the doorway.

Nancy rose to her feet. "Best now that you should sleep."

He went inside, lowered himself to the cot, put his hands under his head, lay staring at the beams.'

Nancy stood looking down at him. "Claude Glystra."

"What?"

"May I come with you?"

He turned his head, stared up in astonishment. "Come where?"

"Wherever you're going."

"Around the planet? Forty thousand miles?"

"Yes."

He shook his head decisively. "You'd be killed with the rest of us. This is a thousand to one chance."

"I don't care . . . I die only once. And I'd like to see Earth. I've wandered far and I know many things . . ." She hesitated.

Glystra put the spur to his brain. It was tired and failed to react. Something was out of place. Would a girl choose such a precarious life from pure wanderlust? Of course, Big Planet was not Earth; human psychology was unpredictable. And yet—he searched her face, was it a personal matter? Infatuation? She colored.

"You blush easily," Glystra observed.

"I'm strong," said Nancy. "I can do as much work as either Ketch or Bishop."

"A pretty girl can cause a lot of trouble."

She shrugged. "There are women everywhere on Big Planet. No one need be alone."

Glystra sank back on the couch, shaking his head. "You can't come with us, Nancy."

She bent over; he felt her breath on his face, warm, moist. "Tell them I'm a guide. Can't I come as far as the forest?"

"Very well. As far as the forest."

She ran outside, into the golden radiance of the day.

Glystra watched her run up the flowered slope. "There goes trouble." He turned his face to the wall.

3

Free For All

He slept an hour, two hours, soaking the rest into his bones. When he awoke, afternoon sunlight was slanting in through the doorway, a flood of richest saffron. Up the slope, the village merry-making was in full swing. Lines of girls and young men, in parti-colored motley like Nancy's, capered back and forth in a dance of light-hearted buffoonery. To his ears came a shrill jig played on fiddles, concertinas, guitars, rhapsodiums. Back, forth, across his vision ran the dancers, bounding in a kind of prancing goose-step.

Pianza and Darrot looked in through the doorway. "Awake, Claude?" asked Pianza.

Glystra swung his feet over the edge of the cot, sat up. "Good as new." He stood up, stretched, patted the back of his head, the soreness had nearly disappeared. "Everything ready?"

Pianza nodded, "Ready to go. We found your ion-shine, also a heat-gun belonging to the mate." He looked at Glystra half-sidewise, an expression of mild calculation on his face. "I understand Nancy has been included in the expedition."

"No," said Glystra, with some irritation. "I told her she might come as far as the forest, that's only two or three hours away."

Pianza looked doubtful. "She's made herself up a pack. Says she's going with us."

Darrot gave his head a terse shake. "I don't like it, Claude." He had a rough baritone voice. It sounded harsh and grating now. "This march is no place for a girl. Bound to be friction, inconvenience."

Darrot's cast of mind was peculiarly grim, thought Glystra. In a conciliatory voice he said, "I'm in full agreement with you. I refused her point blank."

"But she's all packed," said Pianza.

Glystra said tartly, "Well, if she insists on going, if she follows a hundred yards to the rear, I don't see how we can stop her short of physical constraint."

Pianza blinked. "Well, naturally. . . ." His voice trailed off.

Darrot was unconvinced. His square face wore a look of mulish displeasure. "She's travelled widely, she's been to Grosgarth. Suppose she's one of the Bajarnum's secret agents? I understand they're everywhere, even on the other side of the planet, even on Earth."

"It's possible," admitted Glystra. "Anything's possible. For all I know, you work for the Bajarnum yourself. Someone does."

Darrot snorted, turned away.

"Don't worry," said Glystra, slapping him on the shoulder. "When we get to the forest, we'll send her back." He went to the door, stepped outside. Much of his strength had returned, although his legs felt limp and lax.

Pianza said, 'Bishop salvaged the ship's first aid kit, and all his food pills and vitamins. They may be useful; our food won't always be the best."

"Good."

"Cloyville found his camping equipment and we're taking along the stove and the water-maker."

"Any spare power units for the ion-shines?"

"No."

Glystra chewed his lip. "That's bad . . . Find the nun's body?"

Pianza shook his head. "Her cabin is on the bottom."

"Too bad," said Glystra, although he felt little real remorse. The woman had hardly existed as a human being: he had been conscious of a thin white face, a black robe, a black head-dress, an air of intensity, and all was now gone.

Down from the village came the Earthmen, and around them circled the dancers, gay, exalted, aware only of their own motion and color. Ketch, Corbus, Vallusser, Cloyville, Bishop—and Nancy. She stood a little apart, watching the dancing with an air of serene detachment, as if she had renounced whatever ties bound her to Jubilith.

An elder of the village came down the slope, a thin brown man in a heavy loose smock of horizontal brown, gray and white stripes. The rhythm was still in his ears; he jigged to the music following him down the hill.

He spoke to Cloyville, remonstrated; Cloyville pointed to Glystra. The old man jigged to where Glystra stood waiting. He sang out, 'Surely you won't leave us now? The day is at its close; night drifts over the massif and our merriment is not yet upon us."

Glystra held out his arms while Pianza helped him into his pack. He said with a grin, "Dance a couple sets for me."

"You'll be a-dark!"

"We'll be a-dark more times than this once."

"Inauspicious, importunate." He broke into a chant

28

such as children might sing at their games. "The hop-legged sprites abound in the dark; skin to skin they will weld your legs. Bone to bone, flesh to flesh, and all your life shall be hop-step-one, hop-step-one. . . ."

Nancy caught Glystra's eye, shook her head slightly. Glystra turned away, looked out over Big Planet, already flooded in light of a darker gold. Behind him were the dancers in groups of five, wheeling, kicking out their legs at the knee, wagging their heads drolly, and the music waxed shrill and happy. Looking down the vast slope, Glystra suddenly felt weak before the immensity of the journey ahead. Jubilith seemed warm and secure. Almost like home. And ahead—distance. Sectors and sections, extents and expanses. Looking to where Earth's horizon would lie, he could lift his eyes and see lands reaching far on out: pencil lines of various subtle colors, each line a plain or a forest, a sea, a desert, a mountain range . . . He took a step forward, looked over his shoulder. "Let's go."

For a long time the merry music followed their backs, and only when the sun passed behind the slope and mauve dusk came down from the sky did the sounds dwindle to the silence of distance.

The way led across the bracken, a thick resilient mat of gray stalks beaded with dull green nodules. The slope was gentle and uniform, and the coming of Big Planet night brought no difficulties; it was only necessary to walk down the fall of the ground.

Cloyville and Darrot strode together at the head of the group; then came Glystra, with Nancy at one elbow and Pianza at the other. To their left walked Ketch a little apart, and behind came Bishop, eyes on the ground. At the rear, twenty paces behind, walked Corbus, striding easily, and Vallusser, picking his way as if his feet hurt.

Twilight waned and stars appeared. Now there was nothing in the world but darkness, the sky, the breast of the planet and their own infinitesimal persons.

Nancy had been carefully quiet, but now in the dark, she pressed closer to Glystra. Glystra, expecting various wiles and persuasions, grinned to himself and prepared to withstand an assault on his senses.

She spoke in a soft low voice. "Tell me, Claude, which of those stars is Old Sun?"

Glystra scanned the heavens. The constellations were strange and made no particular pattern.

He remembered that on leaving Earth for Big Planet, Cetus was astern till they arrived at Index . . . There, was Spica, and nearby the black bulge of the Porridge Pot. "I think that's the Sun there—right above the bright white star, in toward the big blot of fog."

She stared wide-eyed into the sky. "Tell me about Earth."

"It's home," said Glystra. He looked for several seconds up at the white star. "I'd like to be there . . ."

"Is Earth more beautiful than Big Planet?"

"That's a hard question to answer. Offhand—no. Big Planet is—big. Impressive. The Himalayas on Earth are foothills beside the Sklaemon Range or the Blackstone Cordillera."

"Where are they?" Nancy asked.

Glystra's mind had been wandering. He looked at her blankly. "Where are what?"

"Those mountain ranges? Here on Big Planet?"

"The Sklaemons are about thirty thousand miles north-west, in a part of Big Planet called Matador. The Ski-men live there, I believe. The Blackstone Cordillera is to the southeast, about five thousand miles above the Australian Peninsula, in Henderland."

"There's so much to be learned . . . So many places to see . . ." Her voice broke a trifle. "The Earth-men know more about us than we know ourselves. It isn't fair. You keep us in mental shackles . . ."

Glystra laughed sourly. "Big Planet is a compromise of many people's ideas. Nobody thinks it's right."

"We grow up barbarians," she said passionately. "My father—"

Glystra looked at her quizzically. "A barbarian is not aware that he is a barbarian."

"—was murdered. Everywhere is murder and death. . . ."

Glystra tried to hold his voice at a dispassionate level. "It's not your fault that this is so—but it's not the fault of the Earth people either. We've never attempted to exercise authority past Virginis Reef. Anyone passing through is on his own—and his children pay the price."

Nancy shook her head—a kind of personal little jerk with head cocked sidewise, indicating incomplete conviction.

Glystra tried to think. There was little he could say to her that was concrete and definite. He detested human pain and misery as whole-heartedly as she did. He was equally convinced that Earth could maintain authority only through a finite volume of space. It was likewise impossible to prevent people who so desired to pass the boundaries and declare themselves free of supervision. He also admitted that in such a case, many might suffer from the mistakes of a few. It was an injustice arising from the very nature of human beings. Nancy had known the

31

injustice—the murder, the grief, the anger, the aberrations which reinforcing and building up down the generations, now infected tribes, peoples, races, continents, the entire world. These immediacies would be in the forefront of her mind; his problem was to convey a sense of more-and-less relationships, to endow these vaguenesses and conditionals with enough power to counter the force of her emotion.

"On Earth, Nancy, ever since our first archaic histories, the race has graduated into levels. Some people have lived in complete harmony with their times, others have in their core a non-conformist independence—an apparently built-in trait, a basic emotion like hunger, fear, affection. These people are unhappy and insecure in a rigid society; through all the ages they have been the unclassifiables: the pioneers, explorers, flagpole-sitters; the philosophers, the criminals, the prophets of doom, and the progenitors of new cultural complexes. Akhnaton—Brigham Young—Wang Tsi-po—John D'Arcy. . . ."

They walked on through the dark. The matted bracken crackled underfoot, muffled voices sounded ahead and behind them.

The air was cool and warm at once—balmy, soothing, smelling of a peppery lavender from the bracken.

Nancy, still watching Old Sun, said, "But these people whoever they were, they have nothing to do with Big Planet."

"Jubilith," said Glystra, "was founded by a ballet troupe who apparently desired solitude and peace to perfect their art. Perhaps they only intended to come out for a year or two, but they stayed. The first settlers, almost six hundred years ago, were nudists—people who dislike the wearing of clothes. Convention on Earth forbids

32

nudity. So they bought a ship and went exploring past the edge of the System. They found Big Planet. At first they thought it too big to be habitable—"

"Why should that be?"

"Gravity," said Glystra. "The larger a planet is, the stronger the pull of its gravity. But Big Planet is made of light materials with a specific gravity only a third of Earth's. Earth is a very dense planet, with abundant metals and heavy elements, and so the gravity works out about the same—although there's thirty times the volume here . . . The nudists liked Big Planet. It was paradise—sunny, bright, with a mild climate, and—most essential it had an organic complex similar to that of Earth. In other words Big Planet proteins were not incompatible with Earth protoplasm. They settled here, and sent back to Earth for their friends.

"There was room for other minorities—endless room. Out they migrated—all the cults, misanthropic societies, primitivists, communists, religious monasteries, just people in general. Sometimes they built towns, sometimes they lived by themselves—a thousand, two thousand, five thousand miles from their nearest neighbor. Useful ore deposits are non-existent on Big Planet; technical civilization never had a chance to get started, and Earth refused to allow the export of modern weapons to Big Planet. So Big Planet evolved into a clutter of tiny states and cities, with stretches of open country in between."

Nancy started to speak, but Glystra anticipated her. "Yes, we might have organized Big Planet and given it System law. But—in the first place—it is beyond the established boundaries of the System. Secondly, we would thereby have been defeating the purpose of those people who sacrificed their place on the civilized worlds for independence—a perfectly legitimate aim in itself. Thirdly, we would be denying refuge to other restless souls, with the effect of sending them out seeking other worlds, almost inevitably less propitious. So we let Big Planet become the System's Miscellaneous File. We established Earth Enclave, with the university and trade school, for those who wish to return to Earth. But very few apply."

"Of course not," said Nancy scornfully. "It's forbidden. A place of maniacs."

"Why do you say that?"

"It is well known. Once a Bajarnum of Beaujolais went to the Enclave, he attended the school, and he came back a different man. He freed all the slaves, and stopped all the punishment ordeals. When he declared the land-hold system void, the College of Dukes rose up and killed him, because clearly he was mad."

Glystra smiled wanly. "He was the sanest man on the planet. . . ."

She sniffed.

"Yes," said Glystra. "Very few apply to the Enclave. Big Planet is home. It's free—open—limitless. A man can find any kind of life he wants, even if he may be killed almost any minute. Anyone with Big Planet in his blood never feels loose on the civilized worlds. On Earth and the other planets of the System we have a rigid society with precise conventions. It's smooth and easy now; most of the misfits have gone to Big Planet."

"Dull," said Nancy. "Stupid and dull."

"Not entirely," said Glystra. "After all, there are five billion people on Earth, and no two of them are identical."

Nancy was silent a moment, then, almost as a taunt: "What of the Bajarnum of Beaujolais? He plans to conquer the planet. He's already expanded Beajolais three-fold."

Glystra looked straight ahead, down through the infinite Big Planet night. "If the Bajarnum of Beaujolais or the Nomarch of Skene or the Gaypride Baron or the Nine Wizards or anyone else dominates Big Planet, then the inhabitants of Big Planet have lost their freedom and flexibility even more certainly than if the System organized a federal government. Because then they would be obliged to adapt their lives to aberrations different from their own, and not merely to a few rules and regulations essentially rational."

She was not convinced. "I'm surprised that the System considered the Bajarnum important enough to worry about."

Glystra smiled thinly. "Just the fact of our being here tells you something about the Bajarnum. He's got spies and agents everywhere—including Earth. He regularly violates our number one law—the embargo on weapons and metal to Big Planet."

"A man is killed just as surely with a birkwood sword as with a shaft of light."

Glystra shook his head. "You are considering only one aspect of the subject. Where do these weapons come from? The System prohibits unlicensed manufacture of weapons. It's very difficult establishing a modern factory in secret, and therefore most of the Bajarnum's weapons are stolen or pirated. Ships and depots are ripped open, men killed or herded into slave-bins, bound out for the One-man Heavens."

"One-man Heavens? What are they?"

"Among these five billion I mentioned a minute ago are some very strange people," said Glystra thoughtfully.

"Not all the odd ones have migrated to Big Planet. We have over-rich over-ripe creatures on Earth with too much self-indulgence and not enough conscience. Many of them have found a little world somewhere off in the cluster and set themselves up as gods. The pirates sell them slaves and out on their little domains there's no kind of indulgence or whimsicality they can't allow themselves. After two or three months they return to the System and function as respectable citizens for a period. Then they tire of the cosmopolis, and it's back to their One-man Heaven out in the star-stream."

4

Eight Against an Army

Nancy remained silent. 'What's that got to do with Charley Lysidder?"

Glystra looked at her sidewise, and she saw his face as a white mask in the darkness. "How does the Bajarnum pay for his smuggled weapons? They're expensive. Lots of blood and pain is spent on every ion-shine."

"I don't know . . . I never thought of it."

"There's no metal on Big Planet, few jewels. But there's trade-goods more valuable."

Nancy said nothing.

"Girls and boys."

"Oh. . . ." in a remote voice.

"Charley Lysidder is like a carrier of the plague and he infects half the universe."

"But—what can you do?"

"I don't know—now. Events have not gone according to plan."

"You are only eight men. Futile against the Beaujolais army."

Glystra smiled. "We never intended to fight."

"You have no weapons, no plans, no documents—"

"Just brains."

Nancy subsided into a silence of a quality which caused Glystra to peer at her quizzically. "You're not impressed?"

"I don't know. I'm—very inexperienced."

Glystra once more sought her face through the darkness, this time to make sure she was serious. "We form a team. Each man is a specialist. Pianza here—" he nodded to the gray shape at his left "—is an organizer and administrator. Ketch records our findings on his camera and sonographs. Darrot is an ecologist—"

"What's that?"

Glystra looked ahead to where Cloyville and Darrot walked, and the sound of their footsteps came as a regular double thud-crackle. They were now entering a country clumped with great trees, and ahead loomed the Tsalombar Woods, a line of black heavier than the sky. 'Ecology," said Glystra, "is ultimately concerned with keeping people fed. Hungry people are angry and dangerous."

In a subdued voice Nancy said, "The gypsies are always hungry . . . They killed my father. . . ."

"Cloyville is our mineralogist. I'm coordinator and propagandist." Anticipating her question, he asked, "Why is the Bajarnum able to conquer his neighbors?"

"Because he has a stronger army . . . He's very crafty."

"Suppose his army no longer obeyed him. Suppose no one on Big Planet paid any attention to his orders. What could he do?"

"Nothing. He'd be powerless."

"Propaganda at its maximum effectiveness accomplishes just that. I work with Bishop. Bishop is a student of culture—human society. He can look at an arrowhead and tell you whether the man who made it had six wives or shared a wife with six men. He can study the background of people and discover their racial aberrations, their push-buttons—the ideas that make them react like herds of—" he was about to say "sheep" but remembered that Big Planet harbored no sheep—"herds of pechavies."

She looked at him half-smiling. "And you can make people behave like pechavies?"

Glystra shook his head. "Not exactly. Or I should say, not all the time."

They marched onward down the slope. The trees loomed in closer and they entered Tsalombar Forest. Around him marched eight dark shapes. There were forty thousand miles to travel—and one of these shapes wished him evil. He said under his breath to Nancy, "Someone here—I don't know who—is my enemy. Somehow, I've got to learn who he is. . . ."

She had stopped breathing. "Are you sure?" she asked in a hushed voice.

"Yes."

"What will he do?"

"If I knew, I'd watch for it."

"The Magic Fountain at Myrtleseee could tell you who he is. He knows everything."

Glystra searched his mind. Myrtlesee—a word on a map. "Where's Myrtlesee?"

She gestured. "Far to the east. I've never been there; it's a dangerous journey unless you ride the monoline, and that costs much metal. My father told me of the oracle at the Fountain. He babbles in a frenzy and answers any questions asked and then he dies whereupon the Dongmans select a new oracle."

Glystra was skeptical. "There have been similar oracles on Earth. They are drugged and their ravings are interpreted as prophecy."

"It's rather strange. . . ."

Ahead of them Cloyville and Darrot stopped short. "Quiet!" hissed Darrot. "There's a camp ahead. Fires."

The sighing branches of Tsalombar Forest shut off the sky and the darkness was near-complete. Ahead a tiny spark of red flickered past the ranked tree trunks.

"Would it be the Tree-men?" Glystra asked Nancy.

She said doubtfully, "No . . . They never come down from the trees. And they never build fires; they're deathly afraid of fire . . ."

"Then," said Glystra, "it is probably a party sent out to capture us."

"Or gypsies," said Nancy.

Glystra said, "Everybody come here, close." Dark shapes stepped forward.

Glystra said in a low hurried voice, "I'm going ahead to reconnoiter. I want everyone to stay together. This is emphatic. No one is to move from this group or make a sound until I return. Nancy, you stand at the center; the rest of you stand with your elbows touching. Make sure who is on either side of you, make sure he doesn't move."

He circled the group. "Everybody touching two others? Good. Count off." The names came softly across the darkness.

"I'll be back as soon as possible," said Glystra. "If I need help—I'll yell. So keep your ears open."

The matted bracken crackled under his feet as he stole down the slope.

It was a large fire, a roaring blaze fed by logs, in the center of a clearing. Fifty or sixty men sprawled around the fire, completely at their ease. They wore a loose blue uniform of baggy breeches triced below the knee, smocks gathered at the waist by a black sash. On their chest they wore a red insignia, a triangle apex-down. They carried knives and catapults in their sash; squat baskets heavy with darts hung at their backs. Some of the men wore hats of black felt, bent, twisted, creased in flamboyant flaps and bellies; others went bare-headed with their hats laid nearby on the ground.

They were a rough crew—short and stocky with flat brown faces, little spade beards, narrow-lidded eyes, hooked noses. They had eaten and now were drinking from black kidney-shaped leather sacks. Discipline at the moment was lax.

A little apart, back turned to the noise, stood a man in a black uniform. Glystra saw with unreasonable surprise that it was Abbigens. He conversed with a man evidently the officer-in-charge, apparently instructing him, emphasizing points with motions of his big pale hands. The officer listened, nodded.

Not far from Glystra a train of odd-looking beasts waited restlessly, swinging their long necks, snapping at the air, mumbling and moaning. They were narrow-shouldered, high in the back with six powerful legs and a narrow trustworthy-looking head, a composite of camel, horse, goat, dog, lizard. The driver had not bothered to remove their packs. With sudden interest, Glystra examined the loads they bore.

One carried three metal cylinders, another a squat barrel and a bundle of metal rods. Glystra recognized the mechanism: a knock-down ion-blast, a field-piece capable of smashing Jubilith flat. It was of Earth manufacture, captured in a merciless little skirmish on an outer world, bought in blood, sold for young flesh . . . Glystra looked behind, through the trees, suddenly uneasy. Strange that no sentries had been posted.

A flurry of activity at one side of the clearing caught his attention. A dozen soldiers stood with craned necks, looking up, pointing, talking excitedly. Glystra followed their gaze. A hundred feet overhead was a village—a network of rude trestles, walkways swung on vines, pendant huts swaying like oriole nests. No light showed, the huts were dark, but over the side of the trestles peered several dozen white faces framed in a tousle of brown hair. They made no sound, moved but little, and then like squirrels, quickly, abruptly. Apparently the Beaujolais soldiers had not previously noticed the village. Glystra peered up again. They had found a girl—whey-faced, bleary-eyed, but still a girl. They shouted up taunts and jocularities, to which the tree-men made no response.

Glystra eyed the pack-animals with interest, estimating the chances of leading them into the forest while attention was diverted by the girl in the tree-village. He decided they were scant. Perhaps when they bedded down for the night . . . For the night? Why should they bed down for the night? Jubilith was three or four hours up-slope. More likely they had camped here to await nightfall before venturing out on the moors where they could be seen from the village.

Where the soldiers were baiting the tree-men there was further activity. A young swaggerer with a spike mustache was climbing a rude ladder toward the hut from which hung the head of the slatternly girl. The way was easy; where a branch angled up, steps were cut into the wood. The soldier, spurred by the approving hoots of his comrades, ran up the trunk, paused on a rude platform. Here he was partly veiled by the branches, camouflaged by the flickering firelight shadows. There was a motion, a swishing sound, a thud, a sound of disturbed branches. A sprawling twisting body plunged down from the shadows, landed with a heavy thump.

Glystra jerked back, startled. The event had taken him unaware. He looked up; there was no motion from the tree-village. The faces stared down as before. Apparently the soldier had sprung a trap. A poised weight had swept down, struck him from the platform. Now he lay moaning, writhing. His fellows stood around him, watching dispassionately. There were glances turned up at the tree-men, but without apparent animus or hostility. There was no clamor for revenge, no threats, no fury. The event had occurred; it was fate. . . .

Abbigens and the officer strode over, stood looking down at the fallen man. He choked back his groans, lay silent, staring up white-faced. The officer spoke; Glystra could hear the tone of his voice but could not distinguish the words. The soldier on the ground made a reply, tried to rise to his feet, an anguished effort. But his leg lay out at a curious angle; tilting his chin, gritting his teeth, he lay back.

The officer spoke to Abbigens; Abbigens looked up at the tree-men. They watched from the walkways with wary interest. Abbigens spoke, gesturing up at the tree-village. The officer shrugged, turned aside, made a motion to one of the soldiers, turned away.

The soldier looked down at his comrade on the ground, muttered resentfully. He drew his sword from the sheath, stabbed the fallen man through the chest, the neck, finally up through the eye socket.

Behind the tree Glystra swallowed the lump in his throat. After a moment he was once more able to see the clearing.

The officer strode back and forth through the camp, barking orders, and the words were loud enough for Glystra to hear: 'Up, up on your feet. Form ranks, double-quick, we've overstayed. Driver, see to your beasts—"

Abbigens came forward, spoke briefly to the officer. The officer nodded, crossed the clearing. Glystra could not hear his orders, but the soldier who was tending the pack animals led aside the two beasts bearing the knock-down ion-blast. He removed the packs, assembled the weapon.

Glystra watched with narrow eyes. Was the ion-blast to be used against the tree-village? He looked up. The faces were as before, white blotches peering down from the walkways. One of them looked at him, stared closely a moment, then turned his head back to the clearing without further attention.

The ion-blast was assembled, mounted on its tripod. Firelight glinted on the smooth metal barrel. The cannoneer swivelled the tube back and forth to test the bearing, rocked it up and down checking the balance. He threw off the safety, set the valve, pulled the trigger. A line of violet light lanced from the nozzle, power cracked down the lane of ionized air, spattered into the turf.

Testing. The weapon was ready for use.

The cannoneer set the safety, went to the line of pack-animals, selected the strongest beast, yanked at the straps holding the pack to his back. The driver came forward angrily and the two fell into dispute.

Glystra moved, hesitated, started up, fell back. He gathered himself angrily. Boldness. Take a chance. He stepped forward, heart in mouth, moved out into the firelight. He swung the weapon around, opened the nozzle into a narrow gape, threw off the safety. It was so simple as to be ridiculous.

One of the soldiers noticed him, uttered a sharp cry, pointed.

"Stand still!" Glystra called out in a loud clear voice. "If anyone moves—I'll burn him in two."

5

Capture

Around the clearing shapes froze, startled faces looked in his direction. Yelling in fury, the cannoneer sprang forward. Glystra pulled the trigger; the fan of violet light spread out, power crackled along the conductive air. The cannoneer was shattered and with him five others in the spread of the blaster's fan.

Glystra lifted his voice. "Pianza! Cloyville!"

No reply.

He called again, as loudly as he could, and waited, watching across the sights of the blaster.

None of the soldiers moved. Abbigens stared with his pasty face flat, his eyes like a pair of olives.

There was a rustle of footsteps behind. "Who is it?" asked Glystra.

"Will Pianza—and the rest of us."

"Good. Get around to the side, where you'll be out of range." He raised his voice. "Now—you Beaujolains. Move to the center, this side of the fire . . . *Quick!*" He charged his voice with the push-button crackle of authority.

Glumly the soldiers sidled into the center of the clearing. Abbigens took three quick steps along with them, but Glystra's voice halted him.

"Abbigens—put your hands on your head, walk backwards toward me. Quick, now. . . ."

Glystra said aside to Pianza, "Get his weapon." He snapped to the officer who was quietly shifting toward the rear of the cluster of men. "You—come forward, hands on your head." From the corner of his mouth: "One of you—Corbus—search him."

Corbus stepped forward. Vallusser made as if to follow. Glystra snapped, "You others stand where you are . . . This is ticklish."

Abbigens carried an ion-shine, the officer a rocket-pistol.

Glystra said, "Put the guns on the ground, tie 'em up with pack ropes."

Abbigens and the officer lay helpless. The soldiers stood swaying, muttering in the center of the clearing.

"Nancy," called Glystra over his shoulder.

"Yes,"—in a tight breathless voice.

"Do exactly as I say. Pick up those two weapons—by their barrels. Bring them to me. Don't walk between the blaster and the soldiers. I don't want to kill you."

Nancy walked across the clearing to where the weapons glittered on the ground, bent.

"*By the barrel!*" rasped Glystra.

She hesitated, turned him an odd wide-eyed look, the skin below the ridge of her cheek-bones tight and pale. Glystra watched her stonily. Trust no one. She bent, gingerly picked up the guns, brought them to him. He dropped them into his pouch, looked warily into the faces of his companions. Behind one of the faces was furious scheming . . . Behind which face? Now was a critical moment. Whoever it was would seek to get behind him, pull him away from the blaster . . .

He gestured. "I want all of you to stand over there, to the side." He waited till all his companions stood to the

47

side of the clearing. "Now," he said to the soldiers. "One at a time, cross the clearing . . . "

Half an hour later the soldiers squatted in a tight circle facing inward, a sullen slack-faced group. Abbigens and the officer lay where they had been tied, Abbigens watching Glystra with expressionless eyes. Glystra watched Abbigens also, watched the direction of his glances. Would they seek out his ally?

Pianza looked doubtfully across the clot of prisoners. "This poses quite a problem . . . What are you planning to do with them?"

Glystra standing behind the blaster, relaxed a trifle, stretched. "Well—we can't let them loose. If we can keep the news of this episode away from the Bajarnum, we gain a big head start." Together they surveyed the prisoners, and above the rumpled blue uniforms eyes fearfully reflected back the firelight. "It becomes a choice of killing them or taking them with us."

Pianza snapped his head around in alarm. "Take them with us? Is that—feasible?"

"Down the slope a few miles begins the steppe. Nomad-land. If there's any fighting to be done, perhaps we can persuade them to do it for us."

"But—we have the blaster. We don't need swords and darts."

"What good is a blaster if we're ambushed? Jumped from two or three sides at once? The blaster is a fine weapon when you can see your target."

Pianza shrugged. "It may be difficult to manage them."

"I've considered that. Through the forest we'll tie them together. Once out on the steppes they can march ahead of the blaster. Naturally we'll have to be carefull."

He set the safety on the blaster, nosed the barrel down into the bracken, then strolled to where Abbigens lay. He looked down. "Think it's about time to talk?"

Abbigens drew back the corners of his wide flat mouth. "Sure, I'll talk, What do you want to know?"

Glystra smiled thinly. "Who helped you aboard the *Vittorio?*"

Abbigens looked down the line of faces: Pianza, placid, attentive; the bristling Darrot; Bishop, solemn, a man ludicrously out of place; Ketch; Corbus; Vallusser; and lastly Nancy, standing wide-eyed by Glystra's left elbow.

"Pianza," said Abbigens. "That's the man."

Pianza raised his mild white eyebrows in startled protest. Somewhere else along the line of faces there was a change of expression—a flicker so faint as to be gone even as it manifested itself.

Glystra abruptly turned away. From the corner of his eye he sensed dark shapes disappearing into the trees. The Beaujolais soldiers! How many? Two, three, four? Taking advantage of the Earthman's preoccupation they had slipped across the clearing, disappeared into the woods.

Glystra cursed. If even one got away, the advantage of their head-start was diminished. He snatched the ion-shine from his pouch, slowly replaced it. It would be foolish wasting power on the tree trunks. The footsteps died in the distance, and then there was silence.

Glystra stood still, trying to collect his wits. At the moment there was only one person he was sure of—himself.

He pointed to Darrot and Corbus. "You two man the blaster. Neither of you trust the other. There's an enemy among us, we don't know who he is, and we can't give him the opportunity to destroy us all." He took a step backwards, held his ion-shine ready. "I want to locate the weapons in the crowd. Pianza, you have an ion-shine?"

"Yes. One of Cloyville's."

"Turn your back on me, lay it on the ground."

Pianza did so, without remonstrance. Glystra stepped forward, ran his hand over Pianza's body, into his pouch. He found no other weapon.

In a similar fashion Glystra took the ion-shine from Cloyville, the mate's heat-gun from Ketch. Vallusser and Bishop carried only knives. Nancy carried no weapon of any sort.

Tucking the weapons into his pouch he stepped behind the blaster, took the ion-shine from Corbus. Five ion-shines, counting Abbigens', and the mate's heat-gun.

"Now we're as toothless as possible, and I think we ought to try for some sleep. Ketch, you and Vallusser take a couple of swords, stand on each side of the clearing. Make a triangle with the blaster. Don't get in between the blaster and the soldiers, because if anything happens— you're gone." He turned to Darrot and Corbus. "Hear that? Use that blaster if there's even a hint of an excuse."

"Right," said Corbus. Darrot nodded.

He looked at Nancy, Pianza, Bishop. "We'll try for some sleep now and stand the second watch ... Right there by the fire is a good place, out of range of the blaster."

The bracken was soft and comfortable under the blanket where the firelight had warmed it. Glystra stretched himself down, and fatigue came rising from his bones and muscles, and for an instant he was almost dazed by the pleasant ache of relaxation.

He lay ruminating, hands under his head. Above him

50

the white blotches still peered over the walkways, and for all he could see they had not moved since he had seen them first.

Bishop settled himself nearby, sighed. Glystra eyed him with a moment's pity. Bishop was a student, fastidious, with no natural inclination for roughing it . . . Nancy returned from the forest. Glystra had watched her go with an instant suspicion and then had relaxed. It was impractical to supervise every waking moment of everyone. He must remember, he told himself, to send her home to Jubilith the first thing in the morning. He closed his eyes, opened them a crack. Languor came at him in billows, delightful warmth leaching his consciousness. He lay on his side, one arm thrown over his eyes. It was difficult keeping himself awake.

"Awake or dead," Glystra thought. "Awake or dead." And he forced his eyes open. Darrot, Corbus, Ketch, Vallusser. It was not that he trusted them the less, but that he was instinctively sure of Nancy, Pianza and Bishop.

There was no sound in the clearing other than the low mutter from the cluster of soldiers. Darrot and Corbus stood stiff behind the ionic blaster, Ketch paced slowly along one side of the clearing, Vallusser along the other. Behind him Nancy lay still and warm, Bishop slept like a baby, Pianza tossed fretfully.

All in all, quiet and peaceful. But the air was heavy with someone's private tension—his misgivings, fear, vacillation. The tension permeated the clearing, held Glystra's languor at bay.

The tension grew and Glystra tried to place it objectively. In Corbus' tight alertness, in Darrot's rigidity? In the feel of Nancy at his back? Some subtle wrongness in the breathing of Bishop or Pianza? . . . What had aroused him he could not determine, but he sensed a focus of action forming. As soon as someone could summon the courage. He tried to see whom Abbigens might be watching, without success.

Minutes passed, a quarter hour, a half hour. The air was brittle as ice.

Ketch took a couple of steps toward the blaster, signalled, muttered a few words, backed off into the woods. Glystra watched without seeming to watch as Ketch attended the needs of his body. The soldiers, noting Ketch's momentary preoccupation, reacted with a small ripple of motion. A curt monosyllable from Darrot froze them.

Ketch returned, and now Vallusser stepped into the woods. Again from the captives the quiver of alertness, and again Darrot's soft command and the slow subsidence of blue-clad shoulders, the sinking of the grotesque black felt hats.

A sudden shape behind the blaster, a sweep of sword, a startled cry, a bubble of pure pain . . . Then a stamp of feet, a stabbing flash of steel.

Teeth grinding together, Glystra leapt to his feet, ion-shine in his hand.

At the blaster there was now but one man, crouching, swinging the tube toward Glystra. Glystra saw it coming, saw the elbows tense . . . He squeezed the handle of his ion-shine. Crackling electric streaks down the violet ray. Man's head charred, shriveled; blaster smashed, flung askew. Glystra sprang about facing the soldiers. They had raised to their feet, stood poised, undecided whether to attack or flee.

52

"*Sit down!*" said Glystra, his voice rasping, deadly. The soldiers slumped instantly.

Glystra reached in his pouch, tossed weapons to Pianza, Bishop. "Watch 'em from here; we don't have any more blaster."

He strode to the shattered field weapon. Three bodies. Corbus was still alive. Darrot lay with his dead face turned up, frozen in rage. Vallusser's body, with the head like an oversized black walnut, sprawled across Darrot's legs.

Glystra looked down at the bent little body. "So it was Vallusser the man-hater. I wonder what they bought him with."

Ketch had unpacked the first-aid kit and they knelt beside Corbus. A thrust through the side of his neck was bleeding profusely. Glystra applied a clotting agent, antiseptic and sprayed an elastic film over the wound, which when dry would grip the edges of the cut close together.

He rose to his feet, stood looking down at Abbigens. "Your usefulness is limited. I've found out what I wanted to know."

Abbigens shook the thick yellow hair back out of his face. "Are you going to—kill me?"

"Wait and see." Glystra turned away. He looked at his watch. "Twelve o'clock." He tossed Corbus' ion-shine to Ketch, turned to Pianza and Bishop. "You two sleep; we'll take it till three." He felt alive, refreshed. His enemy had been discovered and dealt with; the pressure of his most immediate problem had been lifted off his mind. Of course, tomorrow would bring new problems . . .

6

The Gypsies

Darrot and Vallusser were buried in a common grave with the Beaujolains: the young swaggerer who had fallen from the tree and the six soldiers who had been killed when Glystra had first seized the blaster.

Abbigens heaved a great sigh when earth began to fall on the bodies. Glystra grinned. Evidently Abbigens had expected to be one with the seven.

Shafts of sunlight, heavy and bright as bars of luminex, prodded down at a slant through the foliage. Pale smoke drifted up from the ashes of the campfire. It was almost time to leave.

Glystra looked around the clearing. Where was Nancy? There she stood, by the pack-beasts, as inconspicuous as she was able to make herself. Behind her the tree-trunks rose like the columns of a great temple, admitting brief glimpses of the sunlit slope.

Nancy felt Glystra's eye, turned him her quick wide glance, with a hopeful hesitant smile. Glystra felt his heart beating. He looked away. Corbus was watching him with an unreadable expression. He compressed his lips, strode forward.

"You'd better be on your way, Nancy—back to Jubilith."

Her smile faded slowly, her mouth drooped, her eyes

became moist. She looked off into the forest. "I'm—afraid," she said in a voice which lacked conviction. "Those soldiers who escaped may be waiting in the forest. . . ."

Glystra snorted. "They're half-way to Montmarchy by now—worse luck. Besides, you can almost see Jubilith from here, straight up the slope. I'm sorry if you're frightened. You can take a catapult and darts if you like. . . ."

She apparently realized the hopelessness of argument, turned away without a word, crossed the clearing. At the edge of the forest she paused, looked over her shoulder.

Glystra watched silently.

She turned away. He watched her a few moments, moving through the trees. He saw her come out on the sunny bracken, listlessly start up the slope toward Jubilith.

Half an hour later the column got under way. The Beaujolains walked single-file, each tied to the man ahead and behind by ankle ropes. They carried their swords and catapults, but the darts were packed in panniers, on one of the pack-beasts.

The officer led the column; Abbigens was the last man. Then came the pack-beasts, with Corbus on a litter between the first two. He was awake and cheerful, and guarded the rear of the column with the big heat-gun.

The village overhead was awake, watching. As the column passed through the forest, the thud of feet sounded along the walkways, along with the creak of fiber fastenings, sometimes a mutter of voices, a child crying. Presently a ceiling of tangled and tattered vegetation, supported by a patchwork of branches, vines and dried yellow fronds, cut off the sunlight. This second floor to the forest spread to a surprising extent, dank on the bottom, trailing bits and shreds of rotting vegetation.

"What do you make of that?" asked Pianza.

"Offhand," responded Glystra, "it looks like a hanging garden . . . We don't have an ecologist with us any more. Darrot probably would have known something about it . . ."

Shafts of sunlight ahead indicated the end of the suspended field. Glystra went to the head of the line, where the officer walked, looked sullenly straight ahead.

"What's your name?" asked Glystra.

"Morwatz. Leg-leader Zoriander Morwatz, 112th at the Champs-Mars Academy."

"What were your orders?"

The officer hesitated, debating the propriety of answering the questions. He was a short man, with a full round face, protuberant black eyes. He spoke in a slightly different dialect than did his soldiers, and carried himself with a trace of self-importance. Apparently he was a warrior by accident of caste rather than inclination, essentially not a bad fellow, Glystra decided. A man like Abbigens would completely overshadow him, reduce him to vacillation and querulousness.

"What were your orders?" repeated Glystra.

"We were placed at the command of the Earthman." He jerked his hand back toward Abbigens. "He carried a cachet from Charley Lyssider, an instrument of great authority."

Glystra digested the information a moment, then asked, "An order addressed to you specifically?"

"To the commanding officer of the Montmarchy garrison."

"Hmmmm." Where had Abbigens obtained this order,

56

signed by the Bajarnum of Beaujolais? There was a pattern here which as yet he was unable to see in the whole. Certainly the fact of Vallusser's guilt did not explain all the events of the last few weeks.

He asked further questions, and learned that Morwatz had been born into the Guerdons, a caste of lesser nobility, and was foolishly proud of the distinction. His home was the village of Pellisade, a few miles south of Grosgarth, and he believed Earth to be the home of a mindless robot race, obeying the sound of gongs and bells like machines. "We'd die here in Beaujolais, before we'd let ourselves be emasculated," declared Morwatz with fine fire.

Here was the obverse, thought Glystra, to the stereotype in Earth minds of the Big Planeter as a flamboyant, reckless creature, totally without restraint. Grinning he asked, "Do any of us look as if our powers of free will were lacking?"

"You're the elite. Here in Beaujolais we have a single lord, Charley Lyssider; never such tyranny as you experience on Earth. Oh, we've heard all about it, from people who know best." He nodded his plump head several times.

Now he looked at Glystra sidelong. "Why do you smile?"

Glystra laughed. "*Naisuka*. The reason that is no reason at all."

Morwatz said suspiciously, "You use an extremely high-caste word. Even I would not feel proper speaking so."

"Well, well," Glystra arched his eyebrows. "You are not allowed to use certain words—but neither do you live under tyranny."

Morwatz pursed his lips. "To be sure the Bajarnum is

a harsh man, but he is conquering the barbarians and forcing them to live correctly."

"And they won't be able to use high-caste words either."

"Precisely. As it should be." And now Morwatz screwed up his courage to ask a question of his own. "And what will you do with us?"

"If you obey orders, you'll have the same chances we have. Frankly, I'm counting on you and your men to protect us on our march. Once we arrive at our destination, your life is your own."

Morwatz said with interest, "Where do you march for?"

"Earth Enclave."

Morwatz frowned. "I don't know the place. How many leagues?"

"Forty thousand miles. Thirteen thousand leagues."

Morwatz faltered in his stride. "You are mad!"

Glystra laughed. "We have the same man to thank for our troubles." He jerked his thumb. "Abbigens."

Morwatz found it difficult to shape his thoughts. "First there is Nomadland and the gypsies. If they capture us, they'll roast us alive and eat us. They are men of a different race and they detest the Beaujolais."

"They won't attack fifty men as readily as they might eight."

Morwatz shook his head despondently. "Last six-moon Heinzelman the Hellhorse raided deep into Beaujolais, and paved the way with the utmost in terror."

Glystra looked ahead through the thinning tree-trunks, to the open slope ahead. "There's Nomadland, ahead of us. What lies beyond?"

"After Nomadland?" Morwatz wrinkled his brow.

"First, the River Oust. And then the swamps, and the Ropemakers of Swamp Island. And after the swamps—"

"What?"

"Directly east, I don't know. Wild men, wild animals. Southerly is the land known as Felissima, and Kirstendale, and the monoline to Myrtlesee Fountain and the oracle. Past Myrtlesee is the Land of Stones, but of this I know nothing, since Myrtlesee is far to the east."

"How many leagues?"

"Several hundred. But it is hard to determine exactly. From here to the river is—five days. To cross you must use the Edelweiss high-line to Swamp Island, or else you must follow the River Oust south-west back toward Beaujolais."

"Why can't we cross the river in boats?"

Morwatz made a wise face. "The griamobots."

"And what are they?"

"Savage river beasts. Horrible creatures."

"Hm. And after the river? What then? How long to cross the swamps?"

Morwatz calculated. "If you journey east, four days—if you find a good swamp car. If you choose to bear southerly, you may take the monoline which leads down past the March—the Hibernian March, that is—to Kirstendale. Possibly six days or a week to Kirstendale. Then, if you're able to leave—"

"Why should we not leave Kirstendale?"

"Some do," said Morwatz with a sly wink. "Others don't . . . From Kirstendale the monoline runs west to Grosgarth, south through the Felissima trade-towns, east to Myrtlesee Fountain."

"How long to Myrtlesee from Kirstendale?"

"Oh—" Morwatz made a vague gesture "—two days,

three days on the monoline. A dangerous trip otherwise, due to the tribesmen down from Eyrie."

"And beyond Myrtlesee?"

"Desert."

"And beyond?"

Morwatz shrugged. "Ask the Magic Fountain. If you are wealthy and pay much metal he will tell you anything you ask." He spoke with confidence.

Glystra thought it might be well to inquire the best way to convey himself and his comrades to Earth Enclave.

Overhead the foliage thinned and the column broke out into the blinding Big Planet sunlight. The slope fell away ahead, a vast windy moor, rolling slightly concave before them. No human habitation or artifact was in sight, but far to the north a dense pillar of smoke bent eastward in the wind.

Glystra halted the column, regrouped the soldiers, arranging them in a square around the pack-beasts—zipangotes, so Morwatz called them. The beast carrying the darts was guarded by Corbus riding in a litter directly behind. He carried a catapult and dart in his hand, with the heat gun tucked inside his shirt secure from any swift clutch. Abbigens walked at the right forward corner, Morwatz at the left rear. Flanking as guards to left and right were Pianza and Cloyville with ion-shines; behind came Bishop and Ketch.

Two hours before noon they set forth across the moor, and as they marched the tremendous slope behind them began to lose its bulk. The upper reaches became murked in the haze, the forest became a dark band. The slope was levelling out into the River Oust pene-plain.

A mutter from the soldiers reached his ears. They were faltering in their step, the whites showed in their eyes.

There was a general nervous motion along the column, a jerking of arms, a tossing of the grotesque black felt hats.

Following their gaze Glystra saw along the horizon a dozen tall hump-backed zipangotes, approaching at a careless pace.

"Who are they? Gypsies?"

Morwatz scanned the column, his face set in rigid lines. "They're gypsies, but not the Cossacks. These are high-caste warriors, possibly even Politburos. Only Politburos ride zipangoes. We can fight off Cossacks, they have little spirit, no discipline, no method, no mind. Only hunger. As soon as there are a few bodies, no matter whose, they are content. But the Politburos . . ." His voice faltered, he shook his head.

Glystra prompted him. "What are the Politburos?"

"They are the great warriors, the leaders. When they appear the gypsies fight like devils. The Cossacks alone are mere robbers. When a Politburo leads them—demons!"

Glystra looked at Bishop. "Know much about these gypsies, Bish?"

"There's a short chapter in Vendome's *Big Planet Lore* on the gypsies, but the emphasis is on their racial background rather than their culture. The stock was originally a tribe of Kirghiz herdsmen from Earth. Turkestan, I believe. When Cloud Control increased trans-Caucasian rainfall, they moved out to Big Planet, where steppes presumably would remain steppes. They shipped out third-class, and in the same hold were a tribe of old-fashioned gypsies and a brotherhood of Polynesians. On the trip out the gypsy leader, one Panvilsap, killed the Kirghiz head-man, married the Polynesian matriarch, and when they were discharged on Big Planet, controlled the entire group. The ensuing culture was mingled Kirghiz, Polynesian and Romany, and dominated by the personality of Panvilsap—an enormous man, a killer, a butcher, as ruthless as he was single-minded."

The column was now less than a mile distant, approaching without haste.

Glystra turned to Morwatz. "How do these people live?"

"They herd zipangotes, hare-hounds, pechavies, milk-rats. They gather fungus from the cycads in Depression. Spring and autumn they raid into Beaujolais and Kerka-ten to the north, Ramspur to the south. The Oust cuts them off from Felissima and the Rebbirs of Eyrie. Ah," sighed Morwatz, "what a grateful war that would be, between the Rebbirs and the gypsies."

"Typical nomadic society," inserted Bishop. "Not a great deal different from the ancient Scythians."

Morwatz said fretfully, "Why are you so interested in the mannerisms of the race? Tonight, they intend to eat us . . ."

7

Heinzelman the Hell-horse

The sun was at zenith, and the coiled gray-green vegetation of the steppe gave off a smoky aroma. As the column approached, it was gradually joined by groups of Cossacks, who fell in behind the slow-jogging zipangotes.

Glystra asked Morwatz, 'Is this their usual method of attack?"

Morwatz yanked at his black headgear. "They observe no usual methods."

Glystra said, "Order your men to take five darts apiece from the pack and stand ready for action."

Morwatz seemed to fill out, expand. His chest and shoulders became rigid, his face tightened. He strode down the front of the square, barking orders. The Beaujolains straightened, formed harder ranks. In groups of five, they passed beside the pack animal which carried the darts, marched back into ranks.

Bishop said dubiously, "Aren't you afraid that—" he paused.

"I'm afraid to act afraid," said Glystra. "They'd be off like jack-rabbits toward the forest. It's a matter of morale. We've got to act as if these gypsies were dirt under our feet."

"I guess you're right—in theory."

The mounted column halted a hundred yards across

the moor, just out of catapult range. The beasts were heavier than those in the pack train—sleek, seal-brown, soft-padded creatures, with ridged convex backs, long heavy necks. They were decked in trappings of shaggy leather painted with crude designs, and each wore a white rhinoceros-like horn strapped to its snout.

A tall burly man sat on the first of the zipangotes. He wore blue satin trousers, a short black cloak, a peaked leather cap with cusped ear-pieces protruding at either side. A three-inch brass ring hung from each ear, and on each side of his chest he wore a medal of polished iron. He had a round muscular heavy-lidded face; his skin was maroon as if charged with a special strong blood.

Glystra heard Morwatz mutter, "Heinzelman the Hellhorse!" And his voice was as flat as if he were reading the hour of his own death.

Glystra re-examined the man, noted his complete ease, an indifferent confidence more striking than any arrogance. Behind rode a dozen others similarly garbed, and still further behind skulked a hundred men and woman in be-ribboned and be-tasselled breeches of dull red, green or blue, heavy fustian blouses, leather skull-caps, some of which were crested by complicated white objects.

Glystra turned to check the formation of the Beaujolains—*thwinggg!* something sang past his throat like a hornet. He recoiled, ducked, looked full in the flat face of Abbigens, lowering his catapult with a curiously black expression.

"Morwatz," said Glystra, "take the catapult from Abbigens, tie his wrists together, hobble him."

Morwatz hesitated a fraction of an instant, then turned, spoke to a pair of soldiers.

There was a scuffle which Glystra ignored—for now

Heinzelman the Hell-horse and his Politburos had dismounted and were approaching.

Heinzelman halted a few paces distant, half-smiling, toying with his quirt. "What is your thought encroaching on the land of the gypsies?" His voice was soft and fluent.

"We're heading for Kirstendale, past the swamps," said Glystra. "The route crosses Nomadland."

Heinzelman drew back his lips, displaying teeth marvellously inlaid with minute bits of colored stone. "You risk your flesh, entering this land of hungry men."

"The risk is to the hungry men."

"From the soldiers?" Heinzelman made a contemptuous gesture. "I will kill each and drink his blood."

Glystra heard a whimper, a cry. "Claude—Claude—"

Hot blood pulsed in his brain. He stood swaying, then became conscious of Heinzelman's amused scrutiny. "Who calls my name?"

Heinzelman looked negligently over his shoulder. "A woman of the slopes we found by the forest this morning. She will be spitted at this evening's camp."

Glystra said, "Bring her forth, I will buy her from you."

Heinzelman said lazily, "Then you have wealth? This is a fortunate day for the gypsies."

Glystra tried to hold his voice steady. "Bring forth this woman or I'll send a man to take her."

"A man? One man?" Heinzelman's eyes narrowed. "What race of man are you? Not Beaujolain, and you are too dark for a Maquir . . ."

Glystra casually brought forth his ion-shine. "I am an electrician." And grinned at his own joke.

Heinzelman rubbed his heavy chin. "In what parts live they?"

"It's not a race; it's an occupation."

"Ah! There are none such among us; we pursue our own business. We are warriors, killers, eaters. And if I gave you the woman, tonight we should go hungry."

Glystra came to a grim decision. He turned his head. "Bring out Abbigens." To Heinzelman: "Electricians carry death in their every gesture."

Abbigens had been thrust forward, and stood still as a pillar, his pale mouth sagging.

Glystra said, "If killing you did not serve a practical purpose, I'd probably march you all the way to Earth Enclave for de-aberration." He raised the ion-shine. Abbigens' face was like risen dough. He began to laugh wildly. "What a joke! What a joke on you, Glystra!" The violet ray snapped out, power crackled down the conductive channel. Abbigens was dead.

Heinzelman appeared faintly bored.

"Give me the woman," said Glystra, "or I'll bring this same death to you. I give you the corpse in her place." He used the push-button rasp of authority. "*Quick!*"

Heinzelman looked up in faint surprise, hesitated, then made a motion to his men. "Let him have her."

Nancy came limping forward, fell shaking and sobbing at Glystra's knees. He ignored her. "Take your meat," he said to Heinzelman. "Go your way and we go ours."

Heinzelman had regained whatever composure he had lost. "I've seen those electrical clubs before. The Bajarnum of Beaujolais brings them down from the sky. But they kill no more certainly than our lances. Especially in the dark, when lances come from many directions and the club points in only one."

Glystra turned to Morwatz. "Give the command to march."

Morwatz stood back, jerked his arm up and down. "Forward!"

Heinzelman nodded, half-smiling. "Perhaps we shall meet again."

The Great Slope was a shadow behind the western haze; the steppe spread as wide as an ocean, carpeted with blue-green bracken except where black-green furze filled the deeper hollows. And behind were the gypsies, a dark clot like flies on stale meat, the Cossacks squatting around the heavier mass of the Politburos on their zipangotes.

In late afternoon a dark shadow appeared in the distance. "Looks like trees, probably an artesian pond," said Cloyville.

Glystra looked around the horizon. "It seems to be the only shelter in sight. We'd better camp for the night." He looked uneasily toward the dark specks in the rear. "I'm afraid we're in for more trouble."

The shadow took on substance, became a copse of a dozen trees. Underneath was a carpet of blue-white moss and lush herbage. A dozen gypsy women scuttled from the shadows, hulking creatures in dirty black robes, to disappear over the lip of a nearby swale. A moment later a flock of fragile white creatures rose up on translucent wings and wheeled down-wind.

At the center of the copse was a small pond bordered by fat rust-colored reeds. A scattering of transparent bubbles, like jellyfish, lay in the mud of the rim. Glystra looked in suspicion at the water, which seemed brackish, but the Beaujolains drank it with relish. Beside the pond was a tall rick full of branches loaded with acorn-like fruit; beside the rick were tubs full of rank beer and a crude still.

The Beaujolains advanced eagerly to investigate the still. Morwatz ran shouting to stop them; reluctantly they turned back.

Glystra took a small cup from one of the packs, gave it to Morwatz. "Serve a measure to each of your men."

There was a whoop of approval and a keg was broached. Glystra said to Pianza, "If we could serve them grog every night we'd never need to guard them."

Pianza shook his head. "Just children. Very little emotional control. I hope they don't become boisterous."

"Liquor or not, we can't relax. You and Cloyville take the first four hours, Bishop, Ketch and I will take the next four. Keep a sharp eye on the beast with the darts." He went to change the bandage on Corbus' neck but found Nancy there before him.

The Beaujolains, singing now, built a fire, and heaping on quantities of the branches from the rick, breathed in the aromatic smoke. Pianza called to Glystra in a worried voice. "They're fighting drunk. I hope they don't get any worse."

Glystra watched in growing apprehension. The Beaujolains were pushing and shouting, trying to shoulder into the densest clouds of smoke, where they stood with faces wreathed in foolish smiles. When they themselves had been pushed aside, immediately they raised angry outcries, cursed, pushed and elbowed a way back into the smoke.

"Must be a narcotic," said Glystra. "Big Planet marijuana. Got to put a stop to it." He stepped forward. "Morwatz!"

Morwatz, red-eyed and flushed from his own indulgence in the smoke, turned a reluctant face to the call.

"Get your men fed and bedded down; enough of the smoke breathing."

Morwatz made a slurred acquiescence, and turning on his men, after a volley of curses, succeeded in bringing order to the camp. A tureen of porridge was prepared—wheat flavored with handfuls of dry meat and fungus.

Glystra went to squat beside Morwatz, where he ate a little apart from his troops. "What is that stuff?" He gestured toward the rick.

Morwatz looked a little sheepish. "It's called zygage—a very potent drug, very valuable." He puffed himself up. "Generally only the lowest castes inhale smoke—very vulgar, the crudest sensations—"

"How do you usually take it then?"

Morwatz breathed heavily. "Normally I do not take it at all. Far too expensive for a warrior. The Mercantils occasionally brew a potion, but its use leads to debility, so I am told. The soldiers will sleep well tonight, so you will observe. Zygage saps much vitality; smoke, potion or nose-salve, the user pays very dearly for his pleasure . . . But look you there, what manner of drug does your man take?"

Glystra turned his head. Bishop was swallowing his customary handful of vitamins.

Glystra grinned. "That's a different kind of drug. It has little effect—makes Bishop think he's healthy. He'd never know the difference if someone fed him chalk."

Morwatz was puzzled. "Another strange and useless Earth custom."

Glystra rejoined his companions. Nancy had served Corbus, then went to sit by herself among the zipangotes, as inconspicuous as possible. Glystra had not spoken to her since she had run to his feet from behind the Politburos.

From the fire came a sudden tumult of hoarse quarrelling. A soldier had quietly cast a new armful of the zygage branches on the flames, and Morwatz had come forward expostulating. The soldier, stumbling and red-eyed, cursed him back.

Glystra sighed. "Now it's discipline. Well—" he rose to his feet "—I suppose we've got to make an example."

Morwatz was pulling the smoking branches from the blaze; the soldier lurched up, kicked him. Morwatz fell face down into the coals.

Cloyville ran forward to pull at the screaming Morwatz; three soldiers leapt on his back, pulled him down. Pianza aimed the ion-shine, but held his fire for fear of shocking Cloyville. Beaujolains came at him from all directions. He aimed, fired: *Snap—snap—snap*. Three soldiers fell flat, shrivelled flesh. The others swarmed over him.

The clearing was suddenly alive with wild-eyed men, screaming and savage. One sprang at Ketch, toppled him. Glystra killed him with his ion-shine, then felt viciously strong arms seize him from behind, hurl him to the ground.

The Earthmen lay weaponless, arms lashed behind their backs.

Nearby Morwatz lay moaning from deep in his throat. The soldier who had first kicked him came forward, a tall man with concave cheeks, a pocked forehead, a split nose. He looked down, and Morwatz regarded him with glazing eyes and moans gradually ascending in pitch. The soldier deliberately drew his sword, punctured Morwatz' neck— once, twice, three times, as if he were prodding a rock.

Morwatz, gurgled, died. He turned, came to look at his captives, tapped Glystra's chin with the reeking sword. He laughed. "Your death will not be at my hands. It's back to Grosgarth for you, and there'll be a reward to set us up as noblemen . . . Let Charley Lyssider have his will with you. . . ."

"The gypsies!' said Glystra in a choked voice. "They'll kill us all!"

"Pah. Dirty animals!" He swung his sword in a wild flourish. "We'll kill them as they come!" He gave a great exultant roar, a wordless drug-addled cry of pure abandon. Leaping to the rick, he threw armful after armful of branches into the blaze. The smoke poured forth, the Beaujolains inhaled it in tremendous racking gulps. Breaking free to gasp for air, they fell to their hands and knees, crawled back to suck up new lungfuls.

Glystra tugged at his bonds, but they had been well-tied, cinched up with no regard for circulation. He craned his neck. Where was Nancy? Nowhere in sight. Had she escaped? Where could she escape to? Glystra ground his teeth. The gypsies would take her and there would be no succor this time . . . Unless she could slip back to the forest during the night. She had clearly fled. The copse was too small to conceal her, and she was nowhere within the range of vision. Twilight was drifting down from the Great Slope—a warm achingly beautiful time of luminous violet air with velvety black and gray shadows below . . . There was a distant sound that he found himself listening to, a far chanting from the steppe, a stave of four notes on a minor scale, punctuated by a rumbling bellow as of a brass horn.

The breeze shifted. Smoke from the smouldering zygage drifted through the rapt soldiers to float across the bound

Earthmen. Twist, turn as they might, avoiding the smoke was impossible. Pungent and sweet, it blossomed up through their nostrils directly into their brains. For a moment they felt nothing; then as one man they lay back, succumbing to the irresistible power of the drug.

The first sensation was double, triple vitality, a thousandfold perceptiveness that saw, heard, felt, smelt with minuscule and catholic exactness. Each leaf on the tree became an identity, each pulse a singular and unique experience. Flitting swarms of pleasant experiences crowded into the mind: triumphs of love, zest of skiing, sailing, space-boating, diving; the joy of colors, the freedom of clouds. At the same time another part of the mind was furiously active; problems beame simplicities; hardships—such as the bonds and the prospect of death at the hands of Charley Lysidder—were details hardly worth attention. And off in the distance the chanting waxed louder. Glystra heard it; surely the Beaujolains must hear it likewise . . . But if they heard it they heeded it not at all.

The breeze shifted again; the smoke drifted away. Glystra felt an instant resentment; he fought his bonds, looked enviously to the Beaujolains standing quiet, quivering slightly in the rapturous smoke.

The chanting was loud, close at hand. The Beaujolains at last heeded. They stumbled away from the fire, black hats askew, eyes bulging, bloodshot, faces distended, mouths gaping and gasping for air.

The leader raised his head like a wolf, screamed.

The cry pleased the Beaujolains. Each one threw back his head and echoed it. Scream after scream of furious challenge rang out toward the gypsies. Now laughing, crying, they loaded themselves with darts, ran out of the copse toward the gypsy horde.

The leader called out; the soldiers, without halting, ordered themselves into a loose formation, and shrilling the eager challenge, charged into the afterglow.

The copse was quiet. Glystra rolled to his knees, struggled to his feet, looked around for means to loosen his bonds. Pianza called in a husky voice, "Stand still; I'll see if I can pull the ropes loose." He rose to his own knees, raised to his feet. He backed against Glystra's hand, fumbled with the thongs.

He gasped in frustration. "My fingers are numb . . . I can't move my hands . . ."

The Beaujolains had crossed the twilight; now the gypsy chanting came to a halt, and only the deep bellow of the horn sounded. Detail was blurred in the evening; Glystra could see men falling, then a convulsive Beaujolain charge which plunged into the gypsies like a knife.

The battle was lost in the dusk.

8

A Matter of Vitamins

Glystra tried to break loose the knots on Pianza's wrists, without success. His fingers were like sausages, without sensation. He was suddenly weak, lax; his brain felt inert. The aftermath of the drug.

The lid to the gypsy still quivered, raised. Dripping, sodden, Nancy looked out—wide-eyed, white-faced.

"*Nancy!*" cried Glystra. "Come here, quick!"

She looked at him as if dazed, moved uncertainly forward, paused, looked out across the steppe toward the melee.

The Beaujolain ululations rose shrill, keen, triumphant.

"Nancy!" cried Glystra. "Cut us loose—before they come back and kill us!"

Nancy looked at him with a strange contemplative expression, as if lost in thought. Glystra felt hopelessly silent. The drugged smoke or the fumes of the still had dulled her reason.

A throbbing chorus of bellows, deep-voiced, rich, rang like bells across the air. There was an intermittent thudding sound, and the Beaujolain yelling choked off, ceased. A voice rose above all others: Heinzelman the Hell-horse. "I kill, I eat your lives! . . . I kill, kill, kill. . . ."

"*Nancy!*" cried Glystra. 'Come here? Untie us! They'll be here any minute. Don't you want to live?"

She sprang forward, took a knife from her sash, cut, cut, cut. Earthmen stood about, rubbing their wrists, grimacing at the pain of restored circulation, torpid with zygage hangover.

Glystra muttered, "At least we need worry no further about guarding the Beaujolains ... A load off our minds. . . ."

"The gypsies will eat well tonight," said Bishop. Alone in the group he appeared alert. Indeed, he was more than alert; he evidently retained the mental edge and physical tone which the others had felt under influence of the zygage. Glystra wonderingly watched him prance up and down, like a boxer loosening his muscles. His own frame felt like a sack of damp rags.

Ketch bent with the effort of an old man, picked up a shining piece of metal. "Somebody's ion-shine."

Glystra searched the clearing, found his own weapon where it had been carelessly flung. "Here's mine ... They were too steamed up to care about anything." The breeze brought a wisp of smoke into his face; new fingers of delight searched into his brain. "*Whew!* That stuff is powerful. . . ."

Bishop had flung himself to the turf and was doing pushups. Feeling the stares of the others he jumped to his feet. "I just feel good," he said, grinning sheepishly. "That smoke did me good."

There was silence from the steppes. Overhead in the pale blue-black sky, stars flickered.

The gypsy war-chant rose up, loud, close at hand. Something whickered overhead, slashing through the leaves.

"Down!" hissed Glystra. "Arrows ... Move away from the fire."

75

Loud came the chant: four notes on a querulous quavering scale, sung with syllables that carried no meaning.

Loud came Heinzelman's voice. "Come forth, you strange men, you miserable intruders, come forth. Come crouch at my feet while I kill you, while I drink your blood; come forth . . . I am Heinzelman the Hell-horse, Heinzelman the life-eater, I eat your life, I am the It, the Pain-maker, Heinzelman. . . ."

They saw his shape silhouetted, and behind him were a string of zipangotes. Glystra sighted along his ion-shine, then hesitated. It was like felling an ancient tree. He called, "You'd do better leaving us alone, Heinzelman."

"*Bah!*" A sound of immeasurable disdain. "You dare not face me higher than your knees. Now I come to kill you; put down your electrical tricks, bow your neck, I come to kill."

Glystra numbly started to lay down the ion-shine, then blinked, fought off the man's magnetism. He pushed the button. Purple sparks flashed at Heinzelman, buried into his chest, absorbed, defeated. "He's grounded!" thought Glystra in sudden panic.

Heinzelman loomed on the afterglow, a heroic figure, larger than life . . . Bishop ran forward, closed with him. Heinzelman bellowed, a ringing bull-sound. He bent, Bishop twisted, rose up beneath. Heinzelman performed a majestic cartwheel, struck earth with a ponderous jar. Bishop sat casually on him, made play with his hands a moment, then stood up. Glystra approached, still numb. "What did you do?"

"Tried out a few judo tricks," said Bishop modestly. "I had an idea the fellow won his battles with his voice, his hypnotic suggestion. Sure enough he was soft; no muscle around his major chord. I killed him dead as a mackerel, one tap in the right place."

"I never knew you were a judo expert."

"I'm not . . . I read a book on the subject a few years back, and it came to me all at once—my word, all those zipangotes!"

"They must have belonged to the other Politburos, that the Beaujolains killed. They're ours now."

"Where are the other gypsies?"

Glystra listened. There was not a sound to be heard across the steppes. A far bray of the horn? He could not be sure.

"They've gone. Melted away."

They returned to the copse leading the zipangotes. Glystra said, "We'd better get going."

Cloyville stared. "Now?"

"Now!" Glystra snapped. He was taut with weariness. "Three Beaujolain soldiers got away last night. They'll take the news to Montmarchy. A new column will be sent out. They'll be mounted on zipangotes, they'll carry metal weapons. We can't take chances. I don't like it any more than you do but—" he pointed to the zipangotes "—at least we can ride."

Morning, midday, afternoon—the Earthmen slumped on the curved backs of the zipangotes, half-dazed with fatigue. The gait was a smooth rocking pitch, not conducive to sleep. Evening came with a slow dimming of the sky.

A fire was built in a hollow, a pot of wheat porridge boiled and eaten, two-hour sentry watches set, and the column bedded down.

Glystra was too tired to fall asleep. He twisted and turned. He thought of Nancy, raised to his elbow. Her eyes were on him. Sweating, he sank back into the couch. It would be hard indulging what he felt to be a mutual passion without making themselves ridiculous. It would also be inconsiderate . . . Sighing, Glystra slumped back into his blankets.

The next morning Glystra opened his eyes to observe Bishop running lightly back and forth along the side of the slope. Glystra rubbed his eyes, yawned, hauled himself to his feet. Feeling dull and liverish he called irritably to Bishop, "What in the world's come over you? I never knew you to go in for early morning exercise before."

A flush mounted Bishop's long homely face. "I can't understand it myself. I just feel good. I've never felt so well in my life. Perhaps my vitamins are taking hold."

"They never took hold before we got all doped up with that zygage. Then they took hold like ice-tongs, and you ran out and played hell with Heinzelman."

"I can't understand it," said Bishop, now half-worried. "Do you think that drug has permanently affected me?"

Glystra rubbed his chin. "If it has it seems to be a good thing—but why did it give the rest of us hangovers? We all ate the same, drank the same . . . Except—" he eyed Bishop speculatively. "I wish we had more of those branches; I'd make some experiments."

"What kind of experiments?"

"It occurred to me that you'd crammed yourself with vitamins—just before the smoke hit us."

"Well, yes. That's true. So I did. I wonder if possibly there's a connection . . . Interesting thought . . ."

"If I ever lay my hands on any more of that zygage," muttered Glystra, watching Bishop absent-mindedly flexing his arms. "I'll find out for sure."

Four days of steady travel passed, from dawn till sunset.

They saw no human being until on the afternoon of the fourth day they came upon a pair of young gypsy girls, perhaps sixteen or seventeen years old, tending a score of sluggish animals, yellow-furred, the size of sheep— pechavies. They wore tattered gray smocks and their feet were tied in rags. The freshness of youth was still theirs, and they had a wild prettiness in no way diminished by their complete fearlessness when they found that the men of the column were not gypsies.

They deserted their animals and ran forward. "Are you slavers," asked the first happily. "We wish to be slaves."

"Sorry," said Glystra dryly. "We're just travellers. Why are you so anxious?"

The girls giggled, eyeing Glystra as if his question were obtuse. "Slaves are fed often and eat from dishes. Slaves may step under a roof when the rain comes, and I've heard it said that slaves are eaten only if no other food is available . . . We are to be eaten this winter, unless the pechavies fatten past expectation."

Glystra looked at them irresolutely. If he set about righting the wrongs of everyone they meet, they would never arrive at Earth Enclave. On the other hand—a stealthy thought—if the other men in the column were provided with women, it would be possible for him to advance his own desires. Of course, camp-followers would slow up the column. There would be added supply problems, emotional flare-ups . . . He looked over his shoulder. Corbus caught his eyes as if divining his thoughts.

"I could use a good slave" he said easily. "You—what's your name?"

"I'm Motta. She's Wailie."

Glystra said weakly, "Anyone else?"

Pianza shook his head. "I'm much too old. Too old."

Cloyville snorted, turned away.

This was embarrassing thought Glystra. Here is where he should display firmness, leadership . . . He passed over Ketch, who gloried in his misogyny, and would suffer the pangs of Saint Anthony before yielding so eaily.

Bishop said tentatively, "I'll take her."

Glystra felt quick relief, vindication of a sort. And the problems of the future could be met as they arose. Now was the present, now was the time containing that sweet union of carbon, oxygen, hydrogen, spirit, will and imagination named Nancy. He met her eyes, as if there had been a signal. She colored faintly, gave an enigmatic jerk of the shoulder, looked away.

Three more days of riding the steppe, each exactly alike. On the fourth day the land changed. The bracken grew taller and harder to ride through, almost like Earthly manzanita. There were occasional flamboyant shrubs six feet tall, with leaves like peacock fans. Ahead appeared a low black blur, which the gypsy girls identified as the bank of the River Oust.

At noon they came upon a fetish post driven into the earth—a round timber eight feet tall, topped by a spherical gourd painted to represent a face.

The gypsy girls made a wide circuit of the post. Wailie said in a hushed voice, "The Magickers of Edelweiss put that there, and only just now, to warn us away from the river."

Bishop patiently pointed out that in all the range of vision there was no living creature but themselves.

"Only just now," declared Wailie stubbornly. "See the moist dirt."

"Does look fresh," Bishop admitted dubiously.

"If you touch the post, you will blacken and die," cried Motta.

Glystra, reflecting that many folk-beliefs were based on fact, searched the steppe in all directions . . . There! A flicker of white? Whatever it was, it disappeared over a distant swale.

In the middle afternoon they came upon Edelweiss, a stockaded fort, with three story blockhouses at each corner.

Motta explained. "Sometimes the South Cossacks raid the Magickers. They are not allowed at the Rummage Sale, because the sight of naked knees drives them mad and they run killing-crazy. But they love the gray powder salt which comes up the river from Gammerei and the Magickers have it in stock, and that is why Edelweiss is girt up with such care."

The town was illumined full-face by the afternoon sun, and across the clear distance appeared as a toy, a miniature, colored dark and light brown, with black windows, light green and black roofs. From the center of town rose a tall pole, with a cupola at the top, like the crow's-nest of a ship.

Motta explained the purpose of the pole. "The high-wire to Swamp Island is made fast at the top of the pole. And then the Magickers always watch the distance; they read the clouds as signs, and the wise hags among them see the future."

"By watching clouds?"

"So it is said. But we know little, being females and raised for use."

They continued to the river, and with the afternoon sun at their backs stood looking over the tremendous Oust. It flowed from the far north, appearing into sight out of the hazy distance, and proceeded into the equally distant south, curving back toward the west. Cat's-paws vibrated the surface, and at intervals came a roiling-up from below, as if a monster fin had set the water into turbulent motion. The other shore, two or three miles distant, was low and flat, and overgrown with a dense forest of tall poles two hundred feet tall. These were silvery-green and stood like stripped and dead tree-trunks or gigantic asparagus shoots. A few blots of color showed at their base—vermilion, blue, yellow—too far distant to be resolved into detail. A long island overgrown with feathery foliage split the center of the river like a wedge.

"Look!" Cloyville cried hoarsely—unnecessarily, for every eye was straining fascinated. Floating from behind the island came a black monster. Its body was round and sleek, its head was like a frog, split by a vast mouth. The head darted forward as they watched, chewed and champed at something in the water, then lowered lazily, lay flat. The creature circled, drifted out of sight behind the island.

Cloyville released his breath. "*Whew!* That's a devilish thing to have for a neighbor."

Pianza searched the face of the river with concern. "I wonder that anyone dares to cross. . . ."

Corbus pointed. "They use the high-line."

It was a thin gray-white cable, swooping from the pole in the village to one of the spines of the forest on the opposite shore. The low point at the center was only fifty feet above the surface of the river.

Glystra snorted in disgust. "They've got the river-crossing sewed up, and so . . . I suppose we'd better apply for transportation."

"That's how the Magickers acquire their wealth," said Motta.

Cloyville muttered, "They'll probably make us pay through the nose. . . ."

Glystra rubbed his short black thatch. "It's a case of take it or leave it. We've got to take it if it breaks us." He looked back across the steppe. "I don't see the Beaujolain's flying squad. No doubt it's there . . . Once we get past the river we can breathe easier. . . ."

They set out along the lip of the bluff toward the village.

Above them towered the walls of Edelweiss, two foot timbers, peeled, set into the ground like piles, lashed at the top with coarse fiber and evidently fastened elsewhere with dowels or tree-nails. The wood appeared punky and soft. Glystra thought that anyone determined on entry could easily chop his way in with a hatchet.

They stopped by the gate, which opened at the rear of a rectangular alcove, well buttressed with extra courses of timber. The gate was open, revealing a short passage walled on either side and cut off at the far end by another wall.

"Strange," said Glystra. "No guards, no gate-keeper . . . In fact—there's no one."

"They're afraid," said Wailie. She raised her strident young voice. "Magickers! Come out and lead us to the high-line!"

There was no overt response. A stealthy rustle sounded behind the walls.

"Come out," yelled Motta, "or we'll burn the walls!"

"My God!" muttered Pianza. Bishop wore an agonized expression.

83

Wailie sought to outdo her companion. "Come out and give us welcome—or it's the sword for all within!"

Bishop clapped his hand over her mouth. "Are you crazy?"

Motta shrieked, "We'll kill the Magickers and burn the Hags, and slide the town into the river!"

There was no motion in the passageway. Three old men, bald, feeble, came forward. Their bare feet were blue-veined and bony, they wore only ragged G-strings, the ribs showed like corrugations down their milk-colored bodies.

"Who are you?" quavered the first. "Go your ways, disturb us not; we have nothing of value."

"We want to cross the river," said Glystra. "Take us across on the high-line and we won't disturb you any further."

The old men engaged in a wheezing colloquy, watching Glystra suspiciously as they whispered. Then: "It is too late in the year. You must wait."

"Wait!" demanded Glystra indignantly. "Out here?"

The eyes of the old men faltered, fell. A muffled voice came from behind the wall. The spokesman cocked his head, listened, then said in a plaintive voice, "We are the quiet Magickers, innocent sorcerers and trades-people. You are men of the Savage Lands, and doubtless you come to loot our valuables."

"The eight of us? Nonsense. We want to cross the river."

There were further instructions from within the wall. The old man said in a quavering voice. "It is impossible."

Glystra lowered his head ominously. "Why?"

"It is forbidden." The old men withdrew. The gate slammed.

Glystra chewed his lip in frustration. "Why in the devil—"

Corbus pointed to the tower. "There's a heliograph up there. It's been shooting signals west. My guess is that they've had orders from the Beaujolains."

Glystra grunted. "In that case, it's more urgent than ever to get across. Here we're trapped."

Cloyville advanced to the bank, peered over. "No boats in sight."

"Not even materials to make a raft," said Pianza.

"A raft wouldn't help us," Cloyville pointed out. "There's no way to propel it, no sails, no sweeps."

Glystra looked up at the walls of Edelweiss. Corbus grinned. "Are you thinking the thoughts I'm thinking?"

"I'm thinking that a piece of that wall—the section running parallel to the river, right there, would make a fine raft."

"But how would we cross the river?" demanded Cloyville. "There's a good current out there; we'd be swept all the way down to Marwan Gulf."

"There's a way staring you in the face." Glystra made a lasso out of a length of pack-rope. "I'm going to climb the wall; you cover me from below."

He tossed the loop around a timber, hauled himself up, cautiously peered over the top, scrambled over.

He looked down. "There's no one up here. It's a kind of roof. One of you come up—Corbus."

Corbus joined him. Behind were blank walls and shielded windows, all silent. Glystra looked skeptically at the windows. "I suppose they're watching, but afraid to show themselves."

85

9

The Griamobot

There was a sound behind them; Ketch hauled himself over the wall. "Thought I'd see what the place looked like." He looked over the flat roofs. "Pretty dingy."

"Notice the wall," said Glystra. "It's lashed along the top with rope, secured along the middle by dowels. If we cut the rope, break the dowels—there, there, there—" he pointed up a vertical crack where the dowels showed through— "and if a man were to shove at each corner, I think we could drop the wall right over into the river."

"How about those sea-serpents—the griamobots?" Ketch asked.

"They're an unknown quantity. We'll have to take a chance."

"They might come up under the raft."

Glystra nodded. "It's a chance. Would you rather stay here?"

"No."

Corbus stretched out his long arms. "Let's get busy."

Glystra looked at the sky. "An hour of light. Enough to get us across, if things go well. Ketch, you go back down, take the whole party, zipangotes and all, down to the beach under the bluff. Naturally, keep clear when things start coming. We'll send the wall down; if it lands in the river, make it fast to the shore, so it won't float away."

Ketch swung himself back down to the ground.

Glystra turned back to the wall. "We've got to get this over before they figure out what we're up to." He looked over the side. Twenty feet below was the edge of the bluff, then another fifty feet, almost straight down, to the beach.

"There won't be any toe-hold to the wall. It should go over almost of its own weight."

"Fifty feet of it ought to be enough," said Corbus. "The wood is light stuff."

"It's not how much we need, it's how much we can get. I don't think they'll stand still when we get to work."

Along the beach below they saw the string of zipangotes, with Ketch, Pianza, Bishop, Cloyville and the three girls.

Glystra nodded to Corbus, drew his knife, slashed at the fiber rope binding the top of the wall. A sudden outraged screeching came from behind. Apparently from nowhere appeared four old women, white creatures with straggling pink-gray hair, howling and gesticulating. A number of Magicker men, lean, white-skinned, daubed around their shoulders with green paint, appeared behind them.

The coarse rope parted. "Now," said Glystra. He aimed his ion-shine, squeezed the button. Once—twice—three times. Three holes down the vertical crack took the place of the pegs. Setting their shoulders to the top of the posts, they pushed out. The wall leaned, creaked, moved no further.

"Below," panted Glystra. "There's more lashings half-way down." He crouched, peered into the dimness under the roof. "We'll have to shoot blind . . . You break your side, I'll do mine."

Two shafts of pale purple light, crackling power. A

tongue of fire licked up the punky side of the timbers, died in a charred smoulder.

The wall sagged, creaked. "Now," panted Glystra, "before they get their army up here . . . Don't go over with it!"

The wall lurched, swept grandly out, fell, landed top-down on the beach, stood a second, sagged outward, slapped into the river with a smash of foam.

Glystra caught a glimpse of Ketch scrambling out with a bit of line, then turned to meet the onrush of a line of the Magickers—gaunt men, naked except for the G-string at their loins. They chattered furiously, but danced back like nervous prize-fighters when they met his eye.

The women screeched, bawled, bellowed, wailed, but the men only made tentative movements forward. Glystra threw a glance down to the river. The wall—now a raft—floated free, pulling at the rope Ketch had made fast. Cloyville and Pianza stood on the shore looking up. Glystra yelled down, "Lead the animals aboard, tie them in the middle."

Bishop called up something Glystra did not catch; he had been distracted by the scene in the room immediately below the roof where he stood, a room now open to the air where the wall had fallen away. Glystra's throat contracted, his stomach twitched . . . Twenty children hung by their hair two feet off the ground. Stone weights were suspended from their feet. Wide-eyed, silent, the children stared from bulging eyes into the new openness, silent except for a hoarse breathing.

"Making tall ones out of short ones," came Corbus' cool voice.

"Look farther down," said Glystra in a low voice. "In the room next lower."

Corbus threw a glance toward the prancing Magickers, peered down under the roof. "Can't see too well . . . It's confused . . . Oh—"

Glystra turned away. The Magickers were stealthily sliding closer. "Get back! Back!" he said flatly. "Or I'll cut your legs out from under you." In a lower voice he said, "I guess it wouldn't make any difference to you if you've all gone through—that. . . ."

But his words were not heard, or if heard, not heeded. Goaded by the frenzied calls of the old women, the Magickers, lips drawn back from their long teeth, were prancing forward, a step at a time. One began to scream—a quavering fierce screech—which the entire line picked up. Suddenly they all were brandishing four-foot pikes tipped with black horny barbs.

"Looks like we'll have to kill a few," said Glystra between tight lips, "unless they'll scare . . ." He aimed the ion-shine at the roof, blasted a hole in the roof at the feet of the nearest Magicker.

The Magicker never shifted his gaze. His eyes had become fixed, saliva bubbled at his mouth.

"They're crazy—hysterics," muttered Glystra. "Poor devils, I don't like it. . . ."

Step by step the Magickers advanced, jerkily, one motion at a time. Behind came the hoarse shrieks of the Hags, and behind—the far glory of Big Planet sunset. Orange, flaring gold.

Too close. Suddenly desperate, Glystra called in a deadly voice, "Two steps more, I'll kill the lot of you. . . ."

One step—two steps—pikes raised in gangling arms.

Glystra squeezed the button. Gaunt forms flapped on the roof.

Hags screamed horror, leapt across the roof to the stairs, black warlock silhouettes, with tatters of cloth flying behind.

Glystra went to the edge, looked over. He yelled down, "Get a line ready, and make it fast to what's coming down next."

Corbus was looking up the pole. "We'd better drop the whole works, pole and all. Otherwise the cable will snap past so fast they won't be able to see it. Notice—three of those guy-lines run to the top, three to the buckle-point at the middle. If we cut off the three at top, the pole should snap off nice and neat."

Glystra examined the magazine of his ion-shine, squinting in the failing light. "Got to go easy on the power. There's not too much soup in this one." He aimed, squeezed the button.

Three gray cables sang, fell twisting like snakes over the roofs of Edelweiss. The pole snapped like a carrot. From the cupola came wild shrieks of fright. "God!" said Glystra. "I'd forgotten all about them. . . ."

The pole crashed almost at their feet; the crying stopped abruptly.

Corbus called over the side, "Here it comes . . . Heads up!"

The tension of the cable dragged the stub across the roof, over the edge of the bluff.

"Lay hold of it!" Glystra yelled. "Make it fast to the raft!" He started to scramble down the wall, past the strung-up children, past the first floor, where he would not look. Corbus was at his heels. They ran along the bluff, found a place to scramble down to the beach.

"Hurry," yelled Pianza. "Our shore line can't take all the strain; it'll go in a minute."

Glystra and Corbus waded out into the river, scrambled up on to the cool soft timbers. "Let 'er go."

The raft drifted free. Behind them the bluff made a black smear across the afterglow, and perched high was Edelweiss, bereft and forlorn with the stump of its broken pole. "Poor devils," said Glystra.

The raft floated out on the river, carried downstream by the current but tethered to the opposite shore by the cable of the broken high-line.

"Ah," sighed Cloyville, dropping his heavy posterior to the logs. "Peace—quiet—it's wonderful!"

"Wait till you get to the other side before you rejoice," said Ketch. "There's still the griamobots."

Cloyville rose swiftly to his feet. "I'd forgotten about them. My Lord! Where are they? . . . If it's not one thing it's another. . . ."

Glystra pointed across the glimmering water to the island—a feathery pyramid sharp on the mauve sky to the southeast. "We won't miss that island far—if at all. And there's not a damn thing we can do about it!"

"Look," said Bishop in a soft voice. Heads turned as if activated by cams, eyes went to the object inching over the edge of the raft—a flat glistening thing, solid and muscular. It quivered, jerked up on the raft another six inches, becoming round in cross-section.

Another six inches . . . Pianza laughed. Bishop moved forward. "I thought it was the end of a tentacle."

"It's a big fluke—some sort of leech or sucker."

"Disgusting thing." Bishop kicked it back into the river.

The raft gave a sudden lurch, swerved, twisted. Domes of water boiled up around them.

91

"Something below," whispered Glystra.

Motta and Wailie began to whimper.

"Quiet!" snapped Glystra. They stifled the sound to a thin whining in their throats.

The motion ceased; the water subsided.

Bishop touched Glystra's arm. "Look up on the Edelweiss cliff."

A torch had appeared. It shone, went out, shone, went out—time and time again for varying intervals.

"Code. They're talking to someone. Probably across the river to Swamp Island. Hope no one cuts the cable at that end."

"Cloyville could swim ashore with a message," suggested Corbus. Cloyville snorted indignantly, and Corbus chuckled.

From behind the island came the griamobot, its head high, questing. The dark concealed its features; evident only were big segmented eyes. Water swished and gurgled past the black hulk of its body, from which came a visceral growling sound.

The head wove, swayed back and forth, suddenly darted forward.

"It sees us," muttered Glystra. He drew his ion-shine. "Perhaps I can damage it or scare it away . . . There's not enough power here for real effect if the brute is determined. . . ."

"Knock the head off," said Pianza tremulously. "Then it won't be able to see us."

Glystra nodded. The violet beam touched the head. It snapped off like a kicked paper bag. But the neck continued to weave, back, forth, back, forth, and the beast never slowed or changed direction.

Glystra aimed at the body, fired. There was a thin

92

ripping sound and a black ragged hole appeared on the dark hide. White objects like viscera seemed to boil up.

Glystra stared, fired again, at the water line. The monster cried out—in a babble of human voices.

The hulk wabbled, wallowed; long white shapes poured out through the hole.

"Duck!" cried Glystra. "They're throwing at us!"

Thud! A pike plunged quivering into the wood beside him. Another—another—then a sound unlike the others: a shock and a long throaty gasp.

Glystra raised up. "*Ketch!*"

Ketch tore feebly at the shaft in his chest, fell forward on his knees, inched yet further forward, bowed his head, with the shaft grasped between his hands, and in this position he froze quiet.

"They're boarding us!" yelled Cloyville.

"Stand aside!" cried Pianza. He elbowed past Cloyville. Lavish plumes of orange flame issued from the heat-gun, wreathed the thin shapes, who threw up their arms, fell backward into the river.

The griamobot hulk had settled low in the water, drifted down-current, past the raft and away.

Glystra gently lay Ketch on his side. His hands were locked on the shaft.

Glystra stood up, looked across the dusk toward Town Edelweiss; then after a moment, turned back to Ketch. "Cloyville—help me."

He lay hold of Ketch's lax ankles. Cloyville bent, took the shoulders, hesitated. "What are you going to do?"

"Drop him in the river. I'm sorry. We can't afford emotion."

Cloyville opened his mouth, stuttered, stammered. Glystra waited.

Cloyville finally said in a subdued voice, "Don't you think we should—well, give him a burial? A decent burial?"

"Where? In the swamp?"

Cloyville bent to the body.

Ketch was gone.

Glystra stood looking up at Town Edelweiss. "The griamobot was a hoax. A commercial enterprise, to frighten people off the river, to funnel them through the Edelweiss high-line. . . ."

Night lay heavy over Big Planet, and the shores were dark. There was silence aboard the raft. Little black waves lapped at the timbers. Down-stream they floated, borne by the current; cross-stream, pulled by the tether of the one-time high-line.

The spines of Swamp Island towered above them. The chirping and rasping of myriad small insects came to their ears. No lights were visible.

The raft bumped gently into a ledge of mud, halted.

"We'll have to wait for light," said Glystra. "Let's try to get some sleep . . ."

But all sat staring across the black water, feeling the loss of dour Ketch as a tongue feels the gap left by a drawn tooth.

The River Oust moved quietly past in the dark, and somewhere now to the south was Ketch.

Dawn came to the water, seeping in from nowhere, moth-colored, the softest luminosity conceivable. First the forest was black and the water black and the sky only less black, then the sky was charged with dimness and the river shone like oil; and then the mother-of-pearl light spread from sky to the air to the river, where it reflected back in odd-shaped leaden plats and planes.

There was more air and water and sky than a man's awareness could encompass. The river's far shore was a low black mark and Town Edelweiss a nubbin on the bluff. The air was still, held in an immense cool quiet, smelling of mud and water and a smoke, spice, early-morning scent, which in all the universe was individual to the one spot here on the shore of the River Oust on Big Planet.

To the east the sky flared orange, yellow, behind the black spines of the Swamp Island forest. They were two hundred feet tall, crowding till in some instances the trunks touched.

Motta screamed, a mindless piping. Glystra swung around; his heart expanded, his blood caked. A tremendous black body blotted out the river, overhead swung a barrel-size head, split by a bony mouth. The head swung down, the eyes stared, the neck looped, the head plunged into the water, returned laden with sodden yellow fiber. It gulped, belched, sank out of sight into the river.

Life returned to the raft. Hysterical women. . . .

Calmness was restored. Glystra released a great pent sigh. "Evidently the griamobots exist."

"I will vouch for it at any time," declared Cloyville.

"But—they're vegetarians. The Magickers arranged that they should be thought carnivorous, and that was all that was necessary to confine river traffic to the high-line . . . Well, let's get moving."

The raft floated flat and vacant on the river. The zipangotes stood loaded and ready on the spongy black humus, raised their feet up and down, swinging their long necks close to the ground.

Glystra walked a little way into the swamp, testing the footing. The round boles, ash-gray overlaid with green luster, prevented a clear vision of more than a hundred feet, but so far as Glystra could see, the ground was uniformly black peat, patched with shallow water. If sight was occluded horizontally, vertically it was wide open; indeed, the upward lines of the trees impelled the eyes to lift along the multitudinous perspectives, up to the little blot of sky above. Walking gingerly across the black bog, Glystra felt as if he were two hundred feet under water, an illusion heightened by the flying creatures, which moved along the vertical aisles with the ease of fish. Glystra saw two varieties: a long electric-green tape with filmy green wings along its body, rippling through the air like an eel, and little puffs of foam drifting with no apparent organs of locomotion.

Glystra returned to the river. The zipangotes had been arranged in line, each long dog-like head under the hindquarters of the beast ahead. "Let's go," said Glystra.

The river fell behind, was quickly lost to sight. The caravan wound like a snake in tall grass—now left, now right, twisting, side-stepping, detouring the puddles of water.

The sun rose, and they rode through shafts and bars of heavy light, and zebra striping lay along the tall spines.

10

The Monoline

About noon, there was a sudden opening before them—a lake. Small waves rippled and glinted at their feet; clouds reflected between areas of deep blue. In the distance floated a few low boats with wide double-lateen booms and baggy orange sails; and beyond was Swamp City. It sat up in the air, on top of the forest, like a mirage; it reminded Glystra of an old-world fishing village.

For several moments the party stood staring at the city on stilts . . . A shrill squawking startled them: a blue and yellow flying thing, beating sluggishly through the air.

"For a moment," said Cloyville, "I thought the Magickers were upon us."

Back to the forest—more winding, squeezing, doubling back, occasionally a straight run of twenty or thirty feet.

The sun moved across the sky; at last, in the middle afternoon, Glystra saw overhead the walls and houses of the city. Five minutes later the caravan moved into the shadow of the deck.

"A moment, please" said an unhurried voice. A platoon of warriors stood beside them, stocky men in mulberry coats.

The officer approached Glystra. "Your business, if you please."

"No business. We're travellers."

"Travellers?" The officer glanced at the zipangotes. "From where?"

"From Jubilith, north of Beaujolais."

"How did you get those beasts across the river? Certainly not on the high-line; our agent would have reported you."

"We ferried them over on a raft. Last night."

The officer fingered his mustache. "Did not the griamobots—"

Glystra smiled. "The Magickers have been hoaxing you. The griamobots are vegetarians, harmless. The only dangerous griamobot was one the Magickers built and filled with soldiers."

The officer swore under his breath. "Lord Wittelhatch will wish to hear this. Magicker regulations and tariffs have long irked him, especially since he strung up the cable to begin with."

"The cable interests me," said Glystra. "Is it metal?"

"Oh no, by no means." The officer laughed affably—a handsome young man with an expressive face and a jaunty straw-colored mustache. "Come, I'll lead you to where your caravan may rest, and along the way you'll see the working of our industry. We are rope-makers to the world; nowhere is cable equal to ours."

Glystra hesitated. "Our wish was to continue as far along the way as possible before nightfall. Perhaps you will direct us—"

"A wealthy man in a hurry," said the officer, thoughtfully eying the three girls, "would ride the monoline. It would cost much metal, much metal . . . Best confer with Wittelhatch."

"Very well." Glystra motioned to the column; they

followed the officer, and a moment later came upon a scene of industry.

A series of rope-walks occupied an area five hundred feet square, which had been partially cleared, leaving only enough spines to support the weight of the city above. Each rope-walk consisted of a series of frames. In the process of formation the rope passed through a hole in the frame and immediately afterward passed through a wheel, which rotated around the rope as an axis. Fixed at regular intervals on the wheel were five fat slugs, and from their positors white strands ran to the rope. As the rope pulled through the frame, the wheel rotated and five new strands were added to the rope.

Glystra sighted up the rope-walk. Each frame had its wheel, and each wheel carried five slugs secreting thread for the rope. "Very clever," said Glystra. "Very clever indeed."

"Our rope is unexcelled," said the officer, with a proud twist for his mustache. "Flexible, weatherproof, strong. We furnish rope for the monolines of Felissima, Bogover, Thelma, also the long line to Grosgarth in Beaujolais and the line out to Myrtlesee Fountain."

"Hm . . . And the monolines are fast transportation?"

The officer inspected him smilingly. "I assure you."

"Just what is a monoline?"

The officer laughed. "Now you joke with me. Come, I will take you to Wittelhatch, and he will doubtless feast you at his evening wassail. I understand an excellent conger bakes in his oven this day."

"But our packs, our luggage! And the zipangotes, they have not eaten yet, there is nothing in this swamp for them to eat!"

The officer signalled; four men stepped forward. "Service and groom the beasts, feed them well, pluck their sores, wash and bind their feet, set them out each a dram of dympel." He said to Glystra. "Your baggage will be secure, Swamp Island knows no thieves. Merchants and industers we be, but robbers no, it is against our rotes."

Wittelhatch was a fat man with round red face, half-petulant, half-jocular, with crafty heavy-lidded eyes. He wore a white blouse embroidered with red and yellow frogs, a red brocade surcingle, tight blue trousers, black boots. In each ear hung a gold ring and each finger was heavy with assorted metals. He sat in a ceremonial chair, apparently having just lowered himself into place, for he was yet wrestling with the folds of his garments.

The officer bowed gracefully, indicated Glystra with a debonair motion. "A traveller from the west, Lord."

"From the west?" Wittelhatch, narrow-eyed, rubbed one of his sub-chins. "I understand that the highline across the river has been cut. It will be necessary to kite it back into place. How then did you cross?"

Glystra explained the Magicker hoax. Wittelhatch became shrill and angry. "The long white muckers—and all the business I've sent them out of pity! Hey, but it discourages an honest community to be set so close to rascals!"

Glystra said with restrained impatience, "Our wish is to proceed on our way. Your officer suggested that we use the monoline."

Wittlehatch immediately became business-like. "How many are in your party?"

"Eight, together with our baggage."

Wittelhatch turned to the officer. "What do you suggest, Clodleberg? Five singles and a pack?"

The officer squinted thoughtfully. "Their baggage is

considerable. Better might be two packs and two singles. And since they are unused to the trolleys, a guide."

"Where is your destination?" Wittelhatch inquired.

"As far east as possible."

"That's Myrtlesee . . . Well now." Wittelhatch calculated. "I care little to let my trolleys journey to such vast extents; you must pay substantially. If you buy the trolleys outright—ninety ounces of good iron. If you rent—sixty ounces, plus the guide's pay and a reasonable return fee—another ten ounces."

Glystra haggled politely, and reduced the rental to fifty ounces plus the zipangotes, and Wittelhatch would pay the guide. "Perhaps, Clodleberg, you would care to lead the party?" Wittelhatch inquired of the young officer.

Clodleberg twisted his blond mustache.

"Delighted."

"Good," said Glystra. "We'll leave at once."

Wittelhatch rang a hand-bell. A porter appeared. "Carry the baggage of these people to the take-off deck."

Wind blew in sails and trolley wheels whispered down the monoline—a half-inch strand of white Swamp Island cable. From the dome at Swamp City the line led from spine to spine across three miles of swamp to a rocky headland, crossed over the rotten basalt with only six feet to spare, swung in a wide curve to the south-east. At fifty-foot intervals L-brackets mounted to poles supported the line, so designed that the trolleys slid across with only a tremor and slight thud of contact.

Clodleberg rode the first trolley, Glystra followed, then came a pair of three-wheel freight carriers loaded with packs—food, spare clothing, the metal which represented their wealth, Bishop's vitamins, Cloyville's camping gear, odds and ends from the Beaujolain packs. The first of the freight-carriers was manned by Corbus, Motta and Wailie; the second by Nancy, Pianza and Bishop. Cloyville in a one-man trolley brought up the rear.

As he examined the vehicle he rode in, Glystra well understood Wittelhatch's reluctance to part with it, even temporarily. The wood was shaped and fitted with painstaking precision, and performed as well as any metal machine from the shops of Earth.

The big wheel was laminated from ten separate strips, glued, grooved and polished. Spokes of hardened withe supported the central hub, whose bearings were wrought from a greasy black hardwood. The seat support was a natural tree-crook, connecting to a slatted floor below. Propulsion was achieved by sails, set to a lateen boom. The halyards, outhauls and sheets led to a cleat-board in front of the seat. Within reach was a double hand-crank, offset like the pedals of a bicycle; turning the crank would drive the trolley up any slight slope at the end of a long suspension which momentum and the pressure of the sails were unable to negotiate.

At noon the land changed. Hills heaved up and it became necessary to make portages, which involved carrying the trolleys and all the baggage up to a higher level of line.

At the end of the day they slept in a vacant cottage near one of the portages and the next morning set off through the mountains—the Wicksill Range, according to Clodleberg. The line swooped far across valleys, from ridge to ridge, with the ground sometimes two thousand feet below. The trolleys, starting out across such a valley, fell into the sag of the cable with a stomach-lifting swoop, falling almost free; then out in the middle the speed would slacken and the trolley would coast on momentum up toward the opposite ridge and presently slow almost to a stop. Then the sail would be trimmed to its fullest efficiency and the drive-crank would be put into use, and gradually the trolley would climb up to the high point.

On the evening of the third day Clodleberg said, "Tomorrow at this time we should be in Kirstendale, and you must be surprised by nothing you see."

Glystra pressed for further information, but Clodleberg was disposed to be jocular. "No, no. You will see for yourself. Kirstendale is a city of great fascination. Possibly you may abandon your fantastic journey and settle in Kirstendale."

"Are the people aggressive, unfriendly?"

"Not in the slightest."

"Who rules them? What is their government?"

Clodleberg raised his eyebrows thoughtfully. "Now that you mention it, I have never heard of a ruler in Kirstendale. Indeed, they rule themselves, if their life could be said to be governed by rule."

Glystra changed the subject. "How many days from Kirstendale to Myrtlesee Fountain?"

"I've never made the trip," said Clodleberg. "It is not entirely pleasant. At certain seasons the Rebbirs come down from the Eyrie to molest the monoline travellers, although the Dongmen of Myrtlesee are Rebbir stock and try to maintain an open avenue of communication."

"What lies past Myrtlesee Fountain?"

Clodleberg made a gesture of disgust. "The desert. The land of fire-eating dervishes; scavengers, blood-suckers, so I'm told."

"And after?"

"Then the Palo Malo Se Mountains and the Blarengorran Lake. From the lake the Monchevior River runs east, and you might float a considerable distance on one of the river boats—how far I am uncertain, because it flows into the obscure and unknown."

Glystra heaved a thoughtful sigh. By the time the Monchevior River floated them out of Clodleberg's ken, there would still be thirty-nine thousand miles to Earth Enclave.

During the night a rainstorm broke upon the mountain, and there was no escape from the roaring wind. The travellers straggled up under the lee of a boulder and huddled under their blankets while the Big Planet gale drove north.

Wet and cold they saw a bleared gray dawn come and for a time the rain stopped, though clouds fleeted past on the wind almost within hand's-reach overhead. Climbing upon their trolleys they set handkerchiefs of sail and scudded along the monoline with wheels whirring.

For two hours the line led along the ridge, and the wind pressed up and over the mountain like a water-spill. The vegetation, low shrubs with tattered blue-green streamers of leaves, whipped and flapped below. To the left was a dark valley full of gray mist, to the right the clouds hid the panorama, but when they broke and parted, a pleasant broken country could be seen—hills, forests, small lakes, and several times they glimpsed great stone castles.

Clodleberg looked back at Glystra, swept his hand over the land to the right. "The Galatudanian Valley, with the Hibernian March below. A land of dukes and knights and barons, stealing each other's daughters and robbing one another . . . Dangerous country to walk afoot."

The wind increased, buffeted the travellers until tears

flew from their eyes, and a fine driven spume stung their cheeks. Heeling far to the side, the trolley skimmed southeast at sixty miles an hour, and they might have travelled faster had not Clodleberg constantly luffed wind from his sails.

For an hour they wheeled along the line, swaying and jerking, and then Clodleberg rose in his seat, signalled to furl sail.

The trolleys costed to a platform from which a line led at a right angle to their course, down into the valley. The far anchor was invisible; all that could be seen was the gradually diminishing swoop of the white cable.

Nancy peered down the line, drew back with a shiver.

Clodleberg grinned. "This is the easy direction. Coming back, a person must make a two-day portage from the valley floor."

"Do we slide down—out there?" asked Nancy in a hushed voice.

Clodleberg nodded, enjoying the trepidation which the prospect of the drop aroused in his charges.

"We'll kill ourselves going so fast; it's so—steep!"

"The wind presses on you, brakes your fall. There's nothing to it. Follow me. . . ."

He turned his trolley down the slanting line, and in an instant was a far dwindling shape vibrating down the wind.

Glystra stirred himself. "I guess I'm next. . . ."

It was like stepping out into nothing, like diving headfirst over a cliff . . . The first mile was almost free fall. The wind buffeted, cloud-wisps whipped past, the land below was an indeterminate blur.

Overhead the wheel sang into high pitch, though it

carried almost no weight. The white line stretched out ahead, always curving slightly up, away, out of vision.

Glystra became aware that the whirr of the wheel was decreasing in pitch; the line was flattening out, the ground below was rising to meet him.

Across a green and yellow forest he rolled and he glimpsed below a settlement of log cabins, with a dozen children in white smocks staring up . . . Then they were gone and the forest was dark and deep below. Flying insects darted up past his eyes, and then ahead he saw a platform hung in the top of a giant tree, and here waited Clodleberg.

Glystra stiffly climbed to the platform. Clodleberg was watching him with a crafty smile. "How did you like the swoop?"

"I'd like to move at that speed for three weeks. We'd be at the Enclave."

The line began to quiver and sing. Looking back up, Glystra saw the freight-carrier with Corbus, Motta and Wailie.

"We might as well start off," said Clodleberg. "Otherwise the platform will be over-crowded." He tested the wind, shook his head. "Poor, a poor reach. We'll have to trim our sails closeby; the wind blows almost down the line . . . However fair winds cannot be ours forever—and I believe the line veers presently to the east, and we'll make better time."

They set off, close-hauled, sailing so near into the eye of the wind that the leach of the sail flapped constantly. The line ran from tree-top to tree-top, and sometimes black-green foliage brushed Glystra's feet . . . Clodleberg had doused his sail, was beckoning him urgently.

"What's the trouble?"

*

Silence, signalled Clodleberg. He pointed ahead. Glystra trundled his trolley forward, up against Clodleberg's. "What's wrong?"

Clodleberg was fixedly watching something on the ground, through a gap in the foliage. "This is a dangerous part of the line . . . Bands of soldiers, starving forest people, bandits . . . Sometimes they wait till a trolley is over a high space, then cut the line, killing the traveller. . . ."

Glystra saw movement through the leaves, a shifting of white and gray. Clodleberg climbed from the trolley into the branches of the tree, let himself cautiously down a few feet. Glystra watched him quietly. Behind came the quiver of the next trolley. Glystra signalled it to a halt.

Clodleberg was motioning to him. Glystra left his trolley, climbed to the crotch where Clodleberg stood. Through a gap in the leaves he could see the floor of the forest. Behind a low orange bush crouched three boys about ten years old. Bows and arrows ready, they watched the line like cats at a mousehole.

"Here's where they get their early training," whispered Clodleberg. "When they grow larger they go to raiding the towns of the March and all the Galatudanian Valley." He quietly nocked a quarrel into his cross-bow.

"What are you going to do?" asked Glystra.

"Kill the biggest . . . I'll be saving the lives of many innocent people."

Glystra struck up his arm; the bolt shattered a branch over the head of the would-be assassins. Glystra saw their white faces, big dark eyes, open frightened mouths; then they were off, scurrying like rabbits.

"Why did you do that?" asked Clodleberg heatedly.

"Those same skulkers may murder me on my way back to Swamp City."

Glystra could find no words at first. Then he muttered, "Sorry . . . I suppose you're right. But if this were Earth, or any of the System planets, they'd be at their schooling."

A shaft of pure brilliance plunged down through the sky—Big Planet sunlight. The rain-washed colors of the forest shone with a glowing clarity never seen on Earth: black-greens, reds, yellows, ochers, buffs, the lime-green of low hangworts, the russet of bundle-bush. The wind blew high, blew low, the clouds flew back across the mountains; they sailed in a fresh sunny breeze.

The monoline dropped down out of the forest, stretched across a river-valley, over a swift river which Clodleberg named the Thelma. They made a fifty foot portage up the opposite bank, and set off once more across a land of peaceful farms and stone houses, undistinguished except for the fact that each house carried on its gable an intricate tangle of brambles and spiny leaves.

Glystra called to Clodleberg. "What on earth are those bristling thorn-patches?"

"Those are the ghost-catchers," said Clodleberg easily. "This section of country abounds with ghosts; there's a ghost for every house, sometimes more; and since they always give a quick jump which takes them to the roof where they can walk back and forth, the traps discourage them sadly . . . The very home of ghosts is this Mankelly Parish, and witches too. . . ."

Glystra thought that no matter how ordinary and uneventful a Big Planet landscape might appear, it was still—Big Planet.

The monoline paralleled a rutted earthen road, and

three times the caravan, swinging along briskly with the breeze on the beam, passed big red farm-wains with six-foot wooden wheels, squeaking and groaning like scalded pigs. They were loaded with red melon-bulbs, bundles of orange vine, baskets of green okra. The lads who walked barefoot alongside goading the longnecked zipangotes wore tall conical hats with veils of white cloth about their faces.

"To fool the ghosts?" Glystra asked Clodleberg.

"To fool the ghosts."

Afternoon wore on; the country became verdant and the ground supported every kind of pleasant growth. The farming region fell behind; they seemed to be traversing a great parkland.

Clodleberg pointed ahead. "See there, that white aquafer? There is your first glimpse of Kirstendale, the finest city of the Galatudanian Valley. . . ."

11

Every Man a Millionaire!

For several minutes little enough of Kirstendale could be seen: splashes of white through the trees, a pair of stone causeways. The trolleys sailed across a pasture of red-green grass, the trees parted, and there was the city, rising from a grassy plain with blue mountains in the background.

It was the largest and most elaborate settlement the Earthmen had seen on Big Planet, but it was never a city which might have existed on Earth. It reminded Glystra of the cloud-borne castles in fairy-story illustrations.

The line took a sudden turn and they came upon a scene of gay activity, carnival color.

A game was in progress. On the field were fifty men and women in garments of remarkable complexity and elegance: silks, satins, velvets, coarse tasselled weaves— tucked, flared, gored, bedecked, be-ribboned, covered with tinsel and lace. The field was laid off into squares by lines of colored grasses, cropped and tended with the nicest precision, and each player occupied a single square. Sheets of silk hung at each side from a row of moored balloons. Each sheet glowed a different color: peach-tan, orange-russet, blue, sea-green, rippling, shining in the breeze. A myriad of small colored balls were in use, balls which half-floated, almost as light as air. The players caught balls in a manner which seemed to depend on the color of the ball, the color of the player's head-ribbon and the square where the player stood. Balls filled the air, little sunlit jewels, and sometimes a player would catch three balls at once and toss them away with great dexterity. When a ball landed in one of the silken curtains, a score was counted to the great jubilation of certain players and spectators who cried, "Ohe, ohe, ohe!"

Several hundred men and women watched the game from the sidelines. They were dressed in the same extravagant fashion, and in addition wore headgear of fantastic complexity, confections most ingeniously designed and assembled. One young man displayed a shell like an overturned boat, striped in bright green and scarlet. Balls of fluorescent blue clung here and there to the fabric, and tapes of golden taupe fluttered below. A great puff of bright purple veil rose from the top, and imbedded in this veil were globes of red, green, blue, yellow, shining like Christmas tree ornaments . . . A young woman—very beautiful, Glystra thought, supple as a kitten, with sleek yellow hair and long yellow eyes—wore first a cloche-helmet of soft leather from which rose a tall antenna, and this antenna radiated prongs tipped with spangles of live fire—vermilion, scintillant green, molten gold. . . . Another—another—another: baroque, unique, incredible . . .

The monoline circled the field. The players and spectators glanced up casually, returned to their game with interest for nothing but the multiple flight of the colored balls.

Glystra noticed an attendant rolling a cart arrayed with pink and white pastries. "Pianza—look what he's wearing . . ."

Pianza snorted in surprise and amusement. "It's a tuxedo. Dinner jacket. Black tie. Stripe down the trousers, patent leather shoes. Wonderful."

Out on the field a ball fell into the billowing russet-gold curtain, rolled softly to the ground. There was joyous applause from the spectators.

Glystra slacked his sails, his trolley coasted quietly along the line. The freight-flat behind, with Pianza and Bishop, overtook him. Glystra spoke over his shoulder, "Bishop, what does the Almanac say about Kirstendale? Anything interesting?"

Bishop came up to stand at the forward end of the flat, under the lead wheel. He looked in frowning reflection toward the looping walls. "Seems as if there's a mystery of sorts—'the Kirstendale Paradox,' that's what they called it. It starts to come back to me. A syndicate of millionaires established the town to beat System taxes. A whole colony came out with their servants—twenty or thirty families. Apparently—well," he waved his hand. "There's the result."

The monoline veered once more, the breeze fell astern. Sails spread out like butterfly wings, the caravan plunged through an arch into the city, coasted up to a landing.

Three quiet men in dark livery came foward, wordlessly removed the packs from the trolley, put them into carts with high spoked wheels. Glystra started to remonstrate, but catching Clodleberg's eye, desisted. "What's happening?"

"They assume that you are wealthy," said Clodleberg, "from the trolleys and the women."

"Humph," grunted Glystra. "Am I supposed to tip them?"

"Do what?"

"Give them money."

Clodleberg blinked, still perplexed.

"Money. Metal."

"Ah, metal!" Clodleberg twisted his natty mustache. "That is as you wish."

The head porter approached, a tall solemn-faced man with carefully shaved cheeks, long sideburns terminating in a little puff of whiskers: a man comporting himself with immense dignity.

Glystra handed him three small iron washers. "For you and your men."

"Thank you, sir . . . And where will you have your luggage sent?"

Glystra shrugged. "What are the choices?"

"Well, there's the Grand Savoyard and the Metropole And the Ritz-Carlton—all excellent, all equally expensive."

"How expensive?"

The head porter blinked, raised his black eyebrows the faintest trifle. "Perhaps an ounce a week . . . The Traveller's Inn and the Fairmont are likewise expensive, but something quieter. . . ."

"What is a good inn of moderate rates?"

The head porter clicked his heels. "I recommend the Hunt Club. This way, sir, to the carriage."

He led them to a landau mounted on four elliptical springs of laminated golden wood. There were no zipangotes hitched to the front, in fact the carriage appeared innocent of motive power.

The head porter swung open the door with a flourish. Cloyville, in the lead, hesitated, looked quizzically back over his shoulder. "A joke? After we get in, do you walk away and leave us sitting here?"

"No indeed, sir, by no means."

Cloyville gingerly climbed up the two steps, lowered himself into the soft seat. The rest of the party followed.

The head porter closed the door with exquisite finesse, signalled. Four men in tight black uniforms stepped forward; each clipped a strap to the front of the carriage, tossed it over his shoulder, and the carriage was underway. Wooden planking rumbled below the wheels, the hangar-like buildings were behind, they drove over granite flags through the heart of the city.

Kirstendale had been laid out with an eye to striking vistas. It was a city clean as new paper, bright with polished stone and glass, gay with flowers. Towers rose everywhere, each circled by a staircase which spiralled up to meet the onion-shaped bulb of the dwelling.

They approached a cylindrical building in the middle of the city, large as a gas-storage tank. A lush growth of blue-green vine with maroon trumpet-flowers, rows of large windows gave a sense of lightness and elegance to an otherwise heavy building.

The carriage passed under a marquee roofed with stained glass, and the Big Planet sunlight, passing through, puddled the flags with gorgeous color. A sign on the marquee read, "Hotel Metropole."

"Hm," said Cloyville. "Looks like a nice place . . . After the—well, inconvenience of the journey, I could stand a week or two in the lap of luxury."

But the carriage continued around the building, presently passed another marquee. This was draped in rich saffron satin, fringed with royal red tassels. A sign read "Grand Savoyard."

Next they passed a portico of somewhat classical dignity: columns, Ionic capitals and entablature. Chiselled letters read "Ritz-Carlton," and again Cloyville looked wistfully over his shoulder as the carriage swept by. "We'll probably end up on a flop-house on the skid-road."

They passed a vaguely Oriental entrance: carved dark wood, a slab of the same wood supporting tall green urns. The sign read, "The Traveller's Inn."

The carriage continued another hundred feet and stopped under an awning of green, red and white striped canvas. A bold black and white sign announced "The Hunt Club."

A doorman stepped forward, helped them to the pavement, then ran ahead, opened the door.

The party of travellers passed through a short corridor pasted with green baize, decorated with black and white landscapes, entered a large central lobby.

Directly opposite, across the lobby, a corridor led outside. Through the door shone the many-colored radiance of stained-glass in the sunlight.

Glystra looked around the walls. At intervals other corridors led off like spokes from a hub, all evidently leading to the outside.

Glystra stopped short. Grinning he turned to Pianza. "The Metropole, the Grand Savoyard, the Ritz-Carlton, the Traveller's Inn, the Hunt Club—they're all the same."

Clodleberg made an urgent motion. "Quiet. This is very real to the Kirsters. You will offend them."

"But—"

Clodleberg said hurriedly, "I should have informed

you; the entrance you chose places you on the social scale. The accommodations are identical, but it is considered smarter and more fashionable to enter through the Metropole."

Glystra nodded. "I understand completely. We'll be careful."

The doorman led them across the lobby to a circular desk with a polished wood counter. Rods wound with spirals of colored cloth rising from the edge of the counter supported a parasol-shaped top. A central pier continued up three feet, then extended in a ten foot pole of pitted black wood. Around the pole, veering in and out, flew ten thousand fireflies—swooping, circling, settling on the pitted wood of the pole, flying out again in a swift current, ten, twenty, fifty feet from the pole.

The doorman took them to that section of the desk marked off by the Hunt Club colors. Glystra turned around, counted heads, like the father of a troublesome family. Cloyville, ruddy and flushed, was talking to a tired Pianza; Corbus and Bishop stood with Wailie and Motta, the girls excited, vastly impressed; Nancy stood pale and rather tense by his right elbow, Clodleberg at his left. Nine in all.

"Excuse me, sir," said the desk clerk. "Are you Mr Claude Glystra, of Earth?"

Glystra swung around in surprise. "Why do you ask?"

"Sir Walden Marchion extends his compliments, and begs that you and your party honor him by residing at his villa the period of your stay. He has sent his carriage for your use, if you will so favor him."

Glystra turned to Clodleberg, spoke in a cold voice. "How did this Sir Walden Marchion know of our arrival?"

Clodleberg flushed, preened his mustaches furiously.

"Who's been talking?"

Clodleberg said with immense dignity, "The head porter at the landing inquired your identity . . . I saw no reason to conceal it. You had issued no orders to that effect."

Glystra turned away. If any harm was to result from the indiscretion, the harm was by now done; no benefit would come of dressing down Clodleberg, for whom, in general, he felt a high regard. "News certainly travels fast in Kirstendale . . . What is your opinion in regard to the invitation?"

Clodleberg turned to the desk clerk. "Exactly who is Sir Walden Marchion?"

"One of the wealthiest and most influential men in Kirstendale. A very distinguished gentleman."

Clodleberg fondled his mustache. "Unusual, but gratifying . . ." He surveyed Glystra with a new appraisal. "I see no reason to decline."

Glystra said to the desk clerk, "We'll accept the invitation."

The desk clerk nodded. "I'm sure that you'll find your visit pleasant. Sir Walden has served meat at his table on several occasions . . . The carriage is awaiting. Ah, Manville, if you will . . ." He signalled to the clerk at the Grand Savoyard sector of the desk. This clerk nodded to a young man in a rich black livery with yellow piping down the sides, who clicked his heels, bowed, stalked out the Grand Savoyard entrance and a moment later reappeared in the Hunt Club corridor. He strode up to Glystra, clicked his heels, bowed.

"Sir Walden's carriage, sir."

"Thank you."

*

Careful not to commit the *faux pas* of leaving by the Traveller's Inn entrance, the party returned outside, climbed into a long low brougham. The doorman closed the door, the carriage driver said, "Your luggage will be conveyed to Sir Walden's."

"Such courtesy," murmured Pianza. "Such unbelievable punctilio!"

Cloyville sank back in the deep cushioned seats with a sigh. "I'm afraid that I like it. Guess I'm soft, or possibly an anachronism. I'll have to admit that all this feudalism finds a customer in me."

"I wonder," said Glystra, watching out the window, "what the desk clerk meant when he said that Sir Walden often served meat."

Clodleberg blew out his cheeks. "Easily explained. By a peculiar freak the Galatudanian Valley supports no animal life other than the zipangotes, whose flesh is so rank as to be inedible. A parasitic insect deadly to creatures with fur, scales or floss is responsible. The zipangote, with his naked hide, is not troubled. The Kirsters therefore subsist on vegetable food, fruits, yeast, fungus, an occasional water-creature, certain varieties of insect, and on rare occasions, meat, imported from Coelanvilli."

The carriage, drawn by five runners in Sir Walden's black livery, trundled across the pavement. They passed a row of shops. The first displayed delicate creations of gauze and puff, the second sold flagons carved of green chert and mottled blue soapstone. The next booth offered pom-poms of twirled green and rose satin, the next was a jewellery, with trays full of glinting lights, next a display of glassware—goblets exceedingly tall and slender, with tiny cups and long fine stems, and the window glittered and glistened in vertical lines and diamond-colored striations.

"I'm rather interested in the economy," said Cloyville. "Somewhere these goods are fabricated. Where? By whom? Slaves? It takes lots of production to support this kind of a set-up. Expensive leisure classes—like that." He pointed to a plaza where men and women in extravagant clothes sat listening to seven young girls playing flutes and singing in clear sweet voices.

Glystra scratched his head. "I don't see how they do it. They certainly can't be supplied from Earth. . . ."

"Evidently this is their secret," said Pianza. "The Kirstendale Paradox."

Cloyville said with an air of finality, "Whatever it is, it seems to suit everybody; everybody seems happy."

"Everybody in sight," said Corbus.

Wailie and Motta had been chattering—bright-eyed, excited. Glystra watched them a moment, wondering what was going on in their brains . . . They had filled out, their cheeks were no longer hollow, their hair was glossy and well-tended, they were pretty girls. Corbus and Bishop were modestly proud of them. Corbus patted Motta's head. "See anything you'd like?"

"Oh, yes! Jewels and metal and lovely cloth, and ribbons and spangles and those lovely sandals. . . ."

Corbus winked at Bishop. "Clothes, clothes, clothes."

"*Le plus de la différence, le plus de la même chose,*" said Bishop.

The carriage turned among the towers—graceful spires swooping up to the onion-shaped dwellings.

The carriage halted by a pale green column; a servant swung wide the door. "The castle of Sir Walden Marchion . . ."

12

Kirstendale Idyll

The party alighted, the carriage swept off.

"This way if you please. . . ."

They climbed the stairs, spiralling up to the beetling shape of Sir Walden's castle. Buttress vanes sprang out from the central column, elbowing up and out to the outer flange.

Corbus felt one of the vanes—a parchment-tan material two inches thick. "Wood . . . Looks like it grows right out of the trunk." He cocked his head up to where the floor swelled out in a smooth curve. "These things grew here! They're big plants!"

The servant looked back, his black brows in a straight disapproving line. "This is the castle of Sir Walden, his manse. . . ."

Corbus winked at Glystra. "Guess I was wrong; it's not a big acorn after all."

"Certainly not," said the servant.

The stairway made one last swoop far out from the central column, apparently supported by its own structural strength; then the party stood on a wide plat, swept by the cool Big Planet breezes.

The servant flung open the door, stood aside. Sir Walden's guests entered the sky-castle.

They stood in a large room, light and airy, decorated

with an unobtrusive intricacy. The floor was not level, but flared like a trumpet bell. A pool of water dyed bright blue filled the depression in the center. Insects with white gauzy wings and feelers scuttled and ran back and forth across the surface, trailing V-ripples which sparkled momentarily green. The floor surrounding the pool was covered by a carpet woven from dark and light-green floss; the walls were bright blue, except where a frieze in sharp black and white, of blank-faced men with owl-insect eyes, occupied one wall.

"Be at your ease," said the servant. "Sir Walden is on his way to welcome you; in the meanwhile dispose yourselves as you will. Refreshing ichors are at your disposal, in three vintages: maychee, worm, vervaine; pray be so good as to enjoy them."

He bowed, withdrew. The travellers were alone.

Glystra sighed heavily. "Looks like a nice place . . . Doesn't seem to be a jail. . . ."

Five minutes passed before Sir Walden appeared—a tall man, sober-faced, rather gravely beautiful. He apologized for not being on hand to greet them, professing himself delayed beyond remedy elsewhere.

Glystra, when he found opportunity, muttered aside to Pianza, "Where have we seen him before? Or have we?"

Pianza shook his head. "Nowhere to my knowledge. . . ."

Two lads of fourteen and sixteen wearing pink, yellow and green, with curl-toed sandals of remarkable design, entered the room. They bowed. "At your service, friends from Mother Earth."

"My sons," said Sir Walden, "Thane and Halmon."

Glystra said, "We are delighted to enjoy the hospitality of your house, Sir Walden, but—bluntly—may I inquire

121

why it has been extended to us, complete strangers that we are?"

Sir Walden made an elegant gesture. "Please . . . We will chat far and long—but now, you are weary and travel-worn. So you shall be refreshed." He clapped his hands. "Servants!"

A dozen men and women appeared. "Baths for our guests scented with—" he kneaded his chin with his hand, as if the matter required the utmost nicety of judgment. He arrived at a decision. "—with Nigali No. 29, that will be most suitable, and let there be new garments for their comfort."

Cloyville sighed. "A bath . . . Hot water. . . ."

"Thank you," said Glystra shortly. Sir Walden's hospitality was still a mystery.

A servant stood before him, bowed. "This way, sir."

He was conveyed to a pleasant chamber high above the city. An expressionless young man in tight black livery took his clothes. "Your bath is through this door, Lord Glystra."

Glystra stepped into a small room with walls of seamless mother-of-pearl. Warm water rose up around his knees, his waist, his chest. Foam, bubbles surged up under his feet, rushed up past his tingling body, burst into his face with a pleasant sharp fragrance. Glystra sighed, relaxed, floated.

The fragrance of the foam shifted, changed, always new, now tart, now sweet. Bubbles kneaded his skin, flushed it free of grime and perspiration, to..ed, stimulated, and fatigue was gone, leaving behind a pleasant soft weariness.

The water level dropped swiftly, warm air gushed around him. He pushed open the door.

The man had disappeared. A girl carrying a towel on two outstretched arms stood before him smiling. She wore a short black skirt, no more. Her body was tan and lovely, her hair arranged in a stylized loose swirl.

"I am your room-servant. However, if you find me unpleasant or unsuitable, I will go."

She seemed very sure that he would find her neither. Glystra stood still a moment, then seized the towel, wrapped himself in it.

"Does—um, everyone get a playmate?"

She nodded.

"The women too?"

She nodded again. "That they may welcome you with renewed pleasure when at last you depart."

"Mmmph," snorted Glystra. He wondered about the man now possibly standing before the naked Nancy. "Mmmph."

He said with a brusqueness and finality he did not altogether feel, "Give me my clothes."

With no change in expression, she brought him Kirstendale garments, assisted him into the intricate folds, tucks and drapes.

At last she pronounced him dressed. He wore a garment of green and blue in which he felt awkward and ridiculous. The first piece of head-gear she brought forward, a tall tricorn dangling a dozen wooden sound-blocks, he refused even to allow on his head. The girl insisted that a man without a head-ornament would be a spectacle for derision, and finally he allowed her to pull a loose black velvet beret over his cropped black poll, and before he could

123

protest she had fixed a string of scarlet beads so as to hang over one ear.

She stood back, admired him. "Now my lord is a lord among lords . . . Such a presence. . . ."

"I feel like a lord among jackasses," muttered Glystra. He went to the door, but the girl was there before him to sweep it open. Glystra frowned, stalked through, wondering if Sir Walden had also arranged to have him fed with a spoon.

He descended to the main hall. Sunset light poured in through the mullioned windows. A pair of lads placed screens of violet and green satin where they would glow to the best advantage. A round table was spread with heavy ivory cloth, and set with fourteen places.

The plates were marble, thin and fragile, apparently carved and worked by hand; the implements were carved from a hard black wood.

One by one Glystra's companions arrived—the men sheepish in their new garments, the girls sparkling and radiant. Nancy wore pale green, pink and white. When she entered the room Glystra hastily sought her eye, hoping to read how she had disposed of the companion assigned her by the painstaking Sir Walden. She looked away, would not meet his eye. Glystra clamped his mouth, scowled toward the blue pool in the center of the room.

Sir Walden appeared and with him his two sons, a daughter, and a tall woman in billows of lavender lace whom he introduced as his wife.

Dinner was a splendid event, course after course, dishes of unfamiliar, odd-tasting food, all elaborately prepared and served: greens, fibers, cereals, fungus, fruits, thistles, succulent stems, prepared in starchy coverings like ravioli, spicy goulashes, croquettes, pastries, jellies, salads. The variety was such that it came as a slight shock when Glystra realized that the meal was entirely vegetarian—with the exception of certain ambiguous hashes, which he took to be of insect origin, and avoided.

After dinner there was oil-smooth liquor and much talk. Glystra's head swam with the dinner wine, and the liquor relaxed him completely. He leaned toward Sir Walden.

"Sir, you have not yet explained your interest in us casual passers-by."

Sir Walden made a delicate grimace. "Surely it is a trivial matter. Since I enjoy your company, and you must rest your heads somewhere—what is the difference?"

"It is a matter which disturbs me," protested Glystra. "Every human act is the result of some impulse; the nature of the impulse which caused you to send the messenger for us preys on my mind . . . I hope you will forgive my insistence. . . ."

Sir Walden smiled, toyed with a bit of fruit. "Some of us here in Kirstendale subscribe to the Doctrine of Illogical Substitution, which in many respects disputes your theory of causation. And then there is the Tempo-fluxion Dogma—very interesting, although I for one cannot entirely accept the implications. Possibly the central postulates are unknown on Earth? The advouters claim that as the river of time flows past and through us, our brains are disturbed—jostled, if you will—by irregularities, eddies, in the flow of the moments. They believe that if it were possible to control the turbulence in the river, it would be possible to manipulate creative ability in human minds. What do you say to that?"

"That I still wonder why you asked us to be your guests."

Sir Walden laughed helplessly. "Very well, you might as well learn the inconsequential truth—and learn the inconsequentiality of our lives in Kirstendale." He leaned forward, as if resolved on candor. "We Kirsters love novelty—the new, the fresh, the exciting. You are Earthmen. No Earthmen have passed through Kirstendale for fifty years. Your presence in my house not only affords me the pleasure of new experience, but also adds to my prestige in the town . . . You see, I am perfectly frank, even to my disadvantage."

"I see," said Glystra. The explanation appeared reasonable.

"I was quick with my invitation. Undoubtedly you would have received a dozen others inside the hour. But I have connections with the depot agent."

Glystra tried to remember the head porter at the landing, who must have relayed the information almost instantly to Sir Walden.

Sir Walden cared little for answering Glystra's questions; he preferred to discuss contemporary Earth culture, a lead which Glystra followed, to please his host.

The evening passed. Glystra, head spinning from the wine and liquor, was conducted to his room. Waiting to undress him was the girl who had helped him into his clothes. She moved on soundless bare feet, murmuring softly as she unclasped the buckles, untied the hundred and one ribbons, bindings, tassels. Glystra was drowsy. Her voice was warm and heady as mulled wine.

The morning attendant was a thin-faced young man, who dressed Glystra after his morning bath in silence.

Glystra hurried to the main hall, anxious to find Nancy. How had she spent the night? The question throbbed at the back of his mind like a bubble of stagnant blood. But she was not yet in evidence. Pianza and Corbus sat alone at the table, eating pink melon.

Corbus was speaking. "—I think I'll trade Motta in on this yellow-haired girl. That's the way to cross a planet, wench by wench!"

Glystra muttered a greeting, sat down. A moment later Nancy entered the room, fresh, blue-eyed, more beautiful than Glystra had ever remembered her. He half-rose to his feet, caught her eye. She nodded casually, dropped into the seat opposite him, began to dip into the pink melon.

Glystra returned to his own food. Big Planet was not Earth. He could not judge a Big Planet girl by Earth standards . . . During breakfast he tried to fathom her mind. She was pleasant, detached, cool.

One by one the party entered the hall, until at last everyone was present. Except—

"Where's Cloyville?" asked Pianza. "Doesn't he plan to get up?" He turned to a servant. "Will you please arouse Mr Cloyville?"

The servant returned. "Mr Cloyville is not in his room."

Cloyville was not seen all day.

It was possible, said Sir Walden, that he had wished to explore the town on foot. Glystra, with no other hypothesis to offer, concurred politely. If Cloyville had indeed wandered off, he would return when he felt so inclined. If he had been taken against his will, Glystra was unable to formulate a plan to retrieve him. Words would avail nothing . . . It might be wise, thought Glystra, to leave Kirstendale as soon as possible. He said as much at lunch.

Wailie and Motta were downcast, and toyed with their

food sulkily. "Best we should remain here in Kirstendale," said Wailie. "Everyone is gay; there is no beating of the woman, and a great deal of food."

"Of course there is no meat," Motta pointed out, "but who cares? The fabrics and the perfumed water and—" she glanced at Wailie and giggled. They looked at Corbus and Bishop, and giggled again.

Bishop blushed, sipped green fruit juice. Corbus raised his eyebrows sardonically. Glystra chuckled; then, thinking of Nancy, asked himself ruefully, what am I laughing at?

Sir Walden said gravely, "I have a rather pleasant surprise for you. Tonight, at our evening meal, there will be meat—a dish prepared in honor of our guests."

He looked from face to face, half-smiling, waiting for the expected enthusiasm. Then: "But perhaps for you, meat is not the gala event it is for us . . . Also, I have been asked to convey the invitation of my Lord Sir Clarence Attlewee to a soiree at his castle this evening. It has likewise been planned in your honor, and he hopes you will accept."

"Thank you," said Glystra. "Speaking for myself, I'll be delighted." He looked around the circle of faces. "I think we'll all be there . . . Even Cloyville, if he shows up."

During the afternoon Sir Walden took them to what he called a "pressing." It proved to be a ceremonial squeezing of essence from a vat of flowing petals. Two hundred of the aristocrats appeared, wearing green and gray headgear, which Sir Walden described as traditional for the occasion.

Glystra looked about the plaza, along the ranks of gay careless faces. "A good proportion of the upper classes

128

must be present, I would imagine," he said idly to Sir Walden.

Sir Walden stared straight ahead, and not a muscle moved on his face. "There are others, many others."

"What is the population of Kirstendale, Sir Walden?"

Sir Walden made a non-committal gesture. "It is at best a speculation. I have no figures."

"And what is your speculation?"

Sir Walden darted him a brilliant glance. "We are a proud race, proud and sensitive. And we have our Secret."

"Excuse me."

"Of course."

The booms which radiated like spokes from the press were bedecked like a maypole, and manned by children. Round and round and round, chanting a shrill song—round and round. Flower fumes rose into the air, and trickle of yellow-green syrup dripped from the spout. Round and round. Essence of white blossoms, lush yellow petals, blue flake-flowers . . . The children bore tiny cups through the crowd, each containing a few drops of essence. Sir Walden said, "Bring your tongue almost to the liquid, but do not quite taste it."

Glystra bent his head, followed the instructions. A wave of pungent fragrance swept through his throat, his nose, his entire head. His eyes swam, his head reeled, momentarily dizzy in a kind of floral ecstasy.

"Exquisite," he gasped when he was able to speak.

Sir Walden nodded. "That was the Baie-Jolie press. Next will be a heavy Purple Woodmint, then a Marine Garden, then a Rose Thyme, and last my favorite, the fascinating Meadow Harvest Sachet."

13

The Secret

Through the afternoon the travellers revelled in perfume, and at last, half-intoxicated from gorgeous odors, they returned to Sir Walden's castle.

Inquiry revealed that Cloyville had not yet returned.

Glystra bathed with a troubled mind. Awaiting him with a towel was the same smiling girl who had served him yesterday. Today she wore, in addition to her short black skirt, a string of red coral beads around her neck.

Sighing, half in frustration, Glystra allowed himself to be arrayed in fresh clothes.

Sir Walden was more attentive and gracious than ever this evening; repeatedly he toasted his guests and planet Earth in wines first green, then orange, then red, and Glystra's head was light before the first series of courses was served.

Course after course: hot pickled fruit, slabs of nutty yeast spread with sweet syrups, salads, croquettes garnished with crisp water-weed—and presently a great tureen was wheeled in, a pottery bowl glazed in stripes of brown, black and green.

Sir Walden himself served the meat—slices of pale roast swimming in rich brown gravy.

Glystra found himself replete, without further appetite, and merely toyed with his portion. Sir Walden and his lady ate with silent concentration, for a moment quiet.

Glystra asked suddenly, "What kind of animal furnishes the meat?"

Sir Walden looked up, wiped his lips with a napkin. "A rather large beast, seldom seen in these parts. It seems to have wandered down from the north woods; by rare luck we procured it; its meat is superlatively delicious."

"Indeed," said Glystra. Looking about he noticed Pianza and Bishop had likewise left their plates untouched. Corbus and Clodleberg still had appetite, and ate the meat with relish, as did Nancy and the gypsy girls.

At the final course—a rich cheese-like substance—Glystra said suddenly, "I think Sir Walden, that tomorrow we will take our leave of Kirstendale."

Sir Walden paused in his eating. "What? So soon?"

"We have far to go, and the monoline takes us but a short distance along the way."

"But—your friend Cloyville?"

"If he is found—" he paused. "If he returns, he possibly may be able to overtake us. I feel that we had better go before—ah, any of us wander away."

"You're spoiling us for the tough life we have ahead," said Pianza. "Another week here and I couldn't bring myself to leave."

Sir Walden politely expressed his regret. "I invited you as curiosities of the moment; now I look upon you as my friends."

A coach came to convey the party to Sir Clarence Attlewee's soiree. Sir Walden stood back.

"But do you not come with us?" asked Glystra.

"No," said Sir Walden. "I will be occupied this evening."

Glystra slowly took his seat in the carriage. Automatically he felt to his side—but he had left his weapon in his room. He whispered to Corbus, "Tonight—don't drink too much. I think that we had better keep our heads clear . . . For what—I don't know."

"Right."

The carriage stopped by a column painted blue-white, and the party was conducted up a spiral staircase much like Sir Walden Marchion's.

Sir Clarence, a man with a heavy chin and snapping eyes, greeted his guests at the head of the stairs. Glystra stared at him. Somewhere, somehow, Sir Clarence's face was familiar to him. He stammered, "Haven't we met, Sir Clarence? This afternoon at the pressing?"

"I think not," said Sir Clarence. "I was otherwise occupied today."

"I feel I've spoken to you before. Your voice is familiar."

Sir Clarence shook his head. "I'm afraid not." He conducted them into his home. "Allow me to present my wife." He did so. "And Valery, my daughter . . ." Glystra's mouth fell open.

Here was the girl who, nearly naked, waited to serve him when he left his bath.

He leaned forward. Or was she? She regarded him with impersonal interest, frowning slightly as if puzzled by his interest. Glystra mumbled, "Charmed to make your aquaintance," and she moved away.

Watching the swing of her body in its complicated wrappings of silk and toile and net, Glystra was certain that she was the same girl.

Bishop nudged him. "There's something rather peculiar—"

"What?"

"Our host Sir Clarence—I've seen him before."

"So have I."

"Where? Do you remember?"

"At the Hunt Club?"

Bishop snapped his fingers. "That's it."

"Who is he?"

"Sir Clarence is—or was—the doorman at the Hunt Club."

Glystra stared, first at Bishop, then at Sir Clarence, who now was speaking with Nancy.

Bishop was right.

Behind him he heard a booming laugh, a great roar of merriment. "Haw, haw, haw! Look at that!"

It was Corbus' laugh, and Corbus laughed only rarely.

Glystra whirled. He looked face to face with Cloyville.

Cloyville wore a black livery, with tiny gold epaulettes. He pushed a cart laden with canapes.

Glystra broke into laughter, as did Bishop and Pianza. Cloyville blushed, a tide of red rising up his bull neck, over his cheeks. He darted an appealing glance toward Sir Clarence, who watched him impassively.

"Well, Cloyville," said Glystra, "suppose you let us in on it . . . Picking up a little spare change during your stay?"

"Care for hors d'oeuvres, sir?" asked Cloyville tonelessly.

"No, damn it. No hors d'oeuvres. Just an explanation."

"Thank you, sir," said Cloyville and rolled his cart away.

Glystra turned to Sir Clarence. "What's going on? What's the joke?"

Sir Clarence wore a puzzled look. "The man is new to my employ. He came to me well recommended—"

Glystra wheeled, strode after Cloyville, who seemed intent on rolling his cart out of the room.

"Cloyville!" barked Glystra. "We're going to thrash this thing out right here."

"Quiet!" hissed Cloyville. "It's not polite to create such a disturbance."

"Thank God I'm not an aristocrat then."

"But I am—and you're hurting my prestige!"

Glystra blinked. "You? An aristocrat? You're just a flunky pushing around a tray of sandwiches."

"Everybody's the same way," said Cloyville dispiritedly. "Everybody works. Everybody is everybody else's servant. How do you suppose they keep up the front?"

Glystra sat down. "But—"

Cloyville said savagely, "I decided I liked it here. I want to stay. I've had enough of tramping across forty thousand miles of jungle, getting killed. I asked Sir Walden if I could stay. He said yes, but he told me I'd have to work like everybody else, and work hard. There's not a more industrious people in space than the Kirsters. They know what they want, they work for it. For every hour of swanking around as an aristocrat they put in two working—in the shops, the factories, in the homes. Usually all three. Instead of living one life, they live two or three. They love it, thrive on it. I like it too. I've decided I'm built the same way. Call me a snob," he shouted, voice rising angrily. "I admit it. But while you and the others are rotting your bones out in the muck I'll be living here like a king!"

"That's all right, Cloyville," said Glystra mildly. "Or perhaps I should say, Sir Cloyville. Why couldn't you tell me of your plans?"

Cloyville turned away. "I thought you'd try to argue with me. Or talk about duty, rot like that—"

"Not at all," said Glystra. "You're a free agent." He turned away. "I wish you luck. I hope you'll like it here. If we ever get to the Enclave I'll send a plane back to pick you up. . . ." He returned to the main hall.

Early the next morning a carriage called at the castle of Sir Walden Marchion. Scrutinizing the men who pulled the carriage, Glystra recognized one of Sir Clarence's sons.

Wailie and Motta were missing. Glystra asked Bishop, "Where's your girl friend?"

Bishop shook his head. "She had breakfast with me."

"Did she know we were leaving?"

"Well—yes."

Glystra turned to Corbus. "How about Motta?"

Corbus looked at Bishop. "Let's face it." He grinned. "We're just not the men these Kirsters are . . ."

Glystra could not prevent himself from glancing swiftly toward Nancy. There she was, pale, rather taut—but there she was. He smiled at her, uncertainly. There was still distance between them.

He turned back to Corbus and Bishop. "Do you want to look for them?"

Corbus shook his head. "They're better off here."

"Let's go," said Bishop.

At the monoline station, the head porter reached into the carriage, unloaded the packs, to a cart, wheeled them to the trolleys.

Glystra winked at his fellows. The porter was Sir Walden Marchion.

135

With a straight face Glystra tipped him once again, three small iron washers.

Sir Walden bowed low. "Thank you very much, sir."

Kirstendale dwindled in the west. As before Clodleberg rode in the lead, with Glystra following. Then came the first freight carrier with Corbus and Nancy, then the second with Bishop and Pianza. Cloyville's trolley had been left behind at Kirstendale.

The party was dwindling. Glystra thought back across the last few weeks. A desperate bloody time. Ketch, Darrot, Vallusser—killed. Cloyville had abandoned the trek. Abbigens, Morwatz, the fifty Beaujolain soldiers—all killed. Heinzelman, the Politburos, the Magickers in the griamobot—killed. A trail of death speading behind like a wake . . . Who would be next?

The thought hung in his mind like a cloud, while they sailed along the bank of a quiet river—the East Fork of the Thelma. The countryside was clumped with Earth-type oaks, cypress, elm and hemlock, imported with the first settlers and now well-adapted; Big Planet flora: bell-briar, mutus weed, handkerchief trees, with flowers like strips of rag, bronzenbush, wire-aspen, a hundred name-less varieties of low jointed furze. Truck-farms and pad-dies occupied the river meadows; the caravan passed neat rows of thistle and legumes, tended by a moon-faced thick-necked people who paid them no heed whatever.

The river presently bore to the north. The monoline continued east, and the country changed. The green meadows and forest became a dark blur to the left and behind; ahead was dry savannah and a range of blue hills in the far Big Planet distance. Clodleberg pointed. "The Eyrie."

*

At noon on the third day Clodleberg pointed ahead once more. "We're coming to Lake Pellitante." Glystra saw the sheen of water, a limpidity in the sky that told of reflection from a large sheet of calm warm water.

The ground became marshy, and presently the monoline swung to the south. For half an hour they crossed dunes sparsely overgrown with dry yellow grass, and the glare off the white sands combined with the normal brilliance of the sunlight made ordinary vision painful.

A high dune passed below, the dry grass licking up at the trolleys like spume at the crest of a wave, and they coasted down toward a lagoon choked with brilliant yellow reeds.

Clodleberg, riding fifty yards ahead, suddenly dropped from sight. The yellow reeds boiled with life; naked men, thin and tall as giraffes, painted in vertical yellow and black stripes, sprang forth. They were immensely tall— eight feet or more—and they came in great bounds. A sharp cry like a bugle-call sounded; the men stopped short, stiffened back to heave spears ... Violet light fanned out, crackling with white sparks. The tall men fell like rags. Three had not been killed, but lay thrashing their long arms and legs like upturned insects.

Clodleberg picked himself up from the ground, stalked across the marsh, stabbed them with their own spears.

The swamp was quiet. Nothing could be heard but a rustle of the breeze in the reeds, the warm hum of insects. Glystra looked at the power-bank of his ion-shine, shook his head. "Done for." He started to toss it to the ground, then remembered the value of metal and tucked it under the seat.

Clodleberg returned to his trolley, still muttering and bristling. "The plague-taken reed-demons, they cut the line!" Evidently, in Clodleberg's register of evils, this was the most depraved crime of all.

"What race are these people?" asked Bishop, who had clambered down one of the line standards to inspect the bodies.

Clodleberg shrugged, and said in a disinterested tone, "They call themselves the Stanezi ... They're a great nuisance to travellers, since they gain nothing from the monoline by way of trade."

Bishop nudged one of the scrawny forms over on its back, peered into the open mouth. "Filed teeth. Hamitic physiognomy ... A Shilluk tribe emigrated to Big Planet from the Sudan about four hundred years ago—an irre-dentist group who chose exile rather than submission to World Government. Very possibly here are their descendants." He looked across the reeds, the dunes, the hot sheen of Lake Pellitante. "The terrain is much like the one they left."

"From the swamps of the Nile to the swamps of Lake Pellitante," apostrophized Pianza.

From the tool-box in his trolley Clodleberg brought a block-and-tackle, and under his direction the broken parts of the monoline were heaved together. Sitting on top one of the standards Clodleberg was able to sink barbed splints into both ends and secure the splice with three whippings of fine cord. Then the tackle was released and the monoline was once more whole.

Clodleberg's trolley was hoisted back up into position; he set his sails and the caravan was once more under way.

As they rounded the elbow of the lagoon Glystra looked back and saw crouching forms steal from the swamp toward the yellow and black-striped bodies ... What a tragedy, thought Glystra. In ten seconds the flower of the tribe wiped out. There would be wailing tonight in the Stanezi village, grovelling in the ashes to the fetishes which had failed them, flagellations, penances. . . .

The monoline took a long gradual slant up into a line of trees bordering Lake Pellitante, and the sudden shade was like darkness. The wind was light, blowing in vagrant puffs, and the trolleys ghosted hardly faster than a man could walk. The lake lay nearly mirror-calm, with a peculiar yellow-gray glisten on the surface, like a film of spider-web. The opposite shore was lost in the haze; far out three or four boats were visible, manned, according to Clodleberg, by fishermen of a tribe who held the land in superstitious dread, and never in the course of their lives set foot ashore.

An hour later they passed a village of house-boats—a triple row of barges floating a hundred yards offshore. The central row was covered with vegetation, apparently a community kitchen garden. There was an air of warmth and contentment to the village, lazy days in the sunlight. . . .

Late afternoon found the party still drifting through the trees of the lake-shore, and at dusk a party of traders appeared, riding the monoline from the opposite direction.

Clodleberg halted his trolley, the lead man in the opposite caravan trundled cautiously closer, and the two exchanged greetings.

The traders were men of Miramar, in Coelanvilli, to the south of Kirstendale, returning from Myrtlesee Fountain. They were bright-eyed wiry men in white linen suits, wearing red kerchiefs around their heads, which detail of dress invested them with a peculiarly piratical air. Clodleberg, however, appeared to be at his ease and Glystra gradually relaxed.

The trade caravan consisted of fourteen freight trolleys loaded with crystallized sugar. By an established rule, the Earthmen, with only four trolleys, were obligated to drop to the ground and allow the traders free-way.

Evening had seeped lavender-gray across the lake, and Glystra decided to camp for the night. The leader of the traders likewise decided to make night camp.

"These are sad times," he told Glystra. "Every hand is turned against the trader, and it is wise to band together as many honest arms as possible."

Glystra mentioned the Stanezi ambush by the lagoon of yellow reeds, and the trader laughed rather weakly.

"The reed men are cowards; they are hardly resourceful or persistent, and run at any loud sounds. It is different on the Palari Desert, where two days ago we escaped the Rebbirs only because a squall of wind drove us at great speed out of danger." He prodded the earth with a stick, looked uneasily to the east. "They are keen as the Blackhelm panthers, as single-minded as fate. It would surprise me not at all to find that a party has followed us down the monoline. For this reason we have kept our sleep short and our sentries double."

14

Treachery

It was still too early for sleep. The traders sat by the fire, busy with a game involving a rotating cage full of colored insects. Nancy sat cross-legged, her dark-fringed eyes wide, the pupils big and black. Pianza sat on a log, paring his fingernails; Bishop was frowning over a small notebook. Corbus leaned back against a tree, his spare body relaxed, his eyes alert, watchful. Clodleberg greased the bearings of the trolleys, humming through his teeth.

Glystra walked down to the shore, to watch evening settle over the lake. Immense quiet enveloped the world, and the faint sounds from the camp only pointed up the stillness. The west was orange, green and gray; the east was washed in tenderest mauve. The wind had died completely. The lake lay flat, with a surface rich as milk.

Glystra picked up a pebble, turned it over in his fingers. "Round pebble, quartz—piece of Big Planet, washed by Big Planet water, the water of Lake Pellitante, polished by the sands of the Big Planet shore . . ." He weighed it in his palm, half-minded to preserve it. All his life it would have the power to recreate for him this particular moment, when peace and solitude and strangeness surrounded him, with Big Planet night about to fall.

Nancy drifted down from among the trees, her hair a mist of pale gold. Thinking of the nights at Kirstendale Glystra felt a pang, a pressure in his throat.

She came close beside him. "Why did you come out here?"

"Just wandering . . . Thinking. . . ."

"Are you sorry you left Kirstendale?"

He was surprised at the tone of wistful reproach. "No, of course not."

"You have been avoiding me," she said simply, looking at him with wide eyes.

Glystra had the uncomfortable feeling he was about to be put on the defensive. "No, not at all."

"Perhaps you found the Kirstendale woman more desirable than me?" Again the tone of sad accusation.

Glystra laughed. "I hardly spoke to her . . . How did you find the Kirstendale man?"

She came close to him. "How could I think of anyone other than you? My mind was full of jealousy. . . ."

The weight lifted from Glystra's mind, the pressure eased from his throat . . . High from the sky came the deep note of a bell, a sonorous vibrating chime. Glystra looked up in astonishment. "What on earth is that?"

"Some kind of night-creature, I suppose."

The note throbbed once more across the lake, and Glystra thought to see a dark shadow sweeping quietly past.

He settled upon a log, pulled her down beside him. "After Myrtlesee there's no more monoline."

"No."

"I've been considering going back to Kirstendale—"

He felt her stiffen, turn her head.

"—and there build a sail-plane large enough to carry all of us. And then I remember that we can't stay aloft indefinitely; that without proper power to keep us going

142

we might as well stay on the ground . . . And then I consider fantastic notions: rockets, kites—"

She caressed his face. "You worry too much, Claude."

"One scheme might work—a balloon. A hot-air balloon. Unfortunately the trend of the wind is south-east, and we would very soon be blown out to sea." He heaved a deep sigh.

Nancy pulled him to his feet. "Let's walk up the shore, where we're farther away from the camp. . . ."

When they returned, the traders had brought out a big green bottle of wine, and all were sitting around the fire, flushed and talkative. Glystra and Nancy each drank a small quantity, and presently the fire tumbled into coals and the night air pinched at their bones.

Sentry watches were arranged, and the party turned into their blankets. Sleep, under the great trees by Lake Pellitante. . . .

Brilliant sunlight flooded the camp. Glystra struggled awake. Why did his mouth taste so vilely? Why had not the last sentry aroused him?

He stared around the camp.

The traders were gone!

Glystra jumped to his feet. Under the monoline lay Pianza, face down—and his neck was ghastly with blood.

The trolleys were gone. Four trolleys, a hundred pounds of metal, clothes, tools. . . .

And Pianza dead . . .

They buried him in a shallow grave in utter silence. Glystra looked up and down the monoline, turned back to his company.

"There's no use fooling ourselves. This is a real blow."

Clodleberg said sheepishly, "The wine—we should never have drunk the wine. They rubbed the inside of our glasses with sleep oil. One should never trust traders."

Glystra shook his head glumly, looked toward Pianza's grave. No more Pianza. It was a real loss. A fine fellow, kind, unassuming, cooperative. A wife and three children awaited his return to Earth, but now they would never see him again. The Earth calcium of his bones would settle into the Big Planet soil . . . He returned back to the silent group.

"Clodleberg, there's no reason for you to come any further. The trolleys are gone, our metal is gone. There's nothing for you ahead. You'd best get back to Kirstendale and pick up Cloyville's trolley, and that should get you back to Swamp City."

There would be Corbus, Bishop, Nancy and himself left in the party. "Any of you others can do likewise. There's hardship and death ahead of us. Anyone who wants to return to Kirstendale—my good wishes go with him."

Nancy said, "Why won't you turn back, Claude? There'll be all our life ahead of us—sooner or later we can get a message to the Enclave."

"No. I'm going on."

"I'll stick," said Bishop.

"I don't like Kirstendale," said Corbus. "They work too hard."

Nancy's shoulders drooped.

"You can go back with Clodleberg," suggested Glystra.

She looked up at him sorrowfully. "Do you want me to?"

"I never wanted you to come in the first place."

She tossed her head. "I'm not going back now."

Clodleberg rose to his feet, twisted his blond mustache.

He bowed politely. "I wish you all the best of luck. You'd be wiser to return to Swamp City with me. Wittelhatch is not the worst master in the world." He looked from face to face. "No?"

"No."

"May you reach your destination."

Glystra watched him as he walked through the trees. His arms swung free. He had left his cross-bow on the trolley; the trolley was gone.

"Just a minute," called Glystra.

Clodleberg turned inquiringly. Glystra gave him the heat-gun. "This should see you past the Stanezi. Throw off the safety here, press this button. There's very little power left in the bank, don't fire it unless it's absolutely necessary."

"Thank you," said Clodleberg. "Thank you very much."

"Goodbye."

They watched him disappear through the trees.

Glystra sighed. "The two or three charges in that gun might have taken us a few extra miles, or killed a few more Rebbirs. It'll save his life . . . Well, let's take an inventory. What's left to us?"

"The commissary packs, with the concentrated foods, my vitamins, our blankets, the water-maker and four ion-shines," said Bishop. "Not very much."

"Makes for easier walking," said Corbus. "Let's get moving. We'll go crazy standing around here moping."

"Good enough," said Glystra. "Let's start."

The lake was forty miles wide—two days march under the quiet trees. On the evening of the second day a river out-flowing from the lake behind the south barred the way, and camp was made on the shore.

Next morning a raft was contrived by cross-piling dead branches. By dint of furious poling and paddling the clumsy construction was forced to the opposite bank, three miles downstream from the monoline.

Climbing up on the bank they looked across the landscape. Looming in the north-east were the crags of the Eyrie, guarded by a wall of great cliffs running north to south.

"Looks like about another three days to the cliffs," said Bishop, "and no perceptible gap for the monoline."

"Perhaps it's just as well we're on foot," said Corbus. "Imagine the portage to the top of the cliff!"

Glystra turned his head, looked along the river bank toward the lake, looked again, squinted. He pointed. "What do you see up there?"

"About a dozen men on zipangotes," said Corbus.

"The traders spoke of a party of Rebbirs . . . Conceivably—" he nodded.

Nancy sighed. "How nice to ride on one of those beasts instead of walking!"

"The same thought had occurred to me," said Glystra.

Bishop said dolefully, "Three months ago I was a civilized human being, never thought I'd turn out a horse-thief."

Glystra grinned. "Makes it less astonishing when you remember that five or six hundred years ago the Rebbirs were civilized Earthmen."

"Well," said Corbus, "what do we do? Walk down and murder them?"

"If they'll wait for us," said Glystra. "I hope we can do

it on less than a macro-watt, because—" he scrutinized the indicator of the ion-shine he had claimed from Pianza's body "—there's only two macro-watts left in the bank."

"About the same here," said Bishop.

"I've got about two good kicks in mine," said Corbus.

"If they ride off peaceably," said Glystra, "we'll know they're good citizens and their lives won't be on our consciences. But if—"

"They've seen us!" cried Nancy. "They're coming!"

It was a race across the stretch of gray plain—men in flapping black cloaks crouched on the thundering zipangotes. These were a species different from the string of beasts they had sold to Wittelhatch; they were larger, heavier, and their heads were bony and white, like skulls.

"Demons!" muttered Nancy under her breath.

The men wore tight helmets of a white shiny substance, ridged over the tip and trailing scarlet plumes behind. Crouched low, knees clamped into the horny black sides of their skull-headed chargers, the foremost flourished swords of gleaming metal.

"Up here, up on the bank," said Glystra. "We want to delay the front ones till they're all within range. . . ."

The horny feet thudded furiously across the plain, the Rebbirs sang out calls of the wildest exultation. The faces of the foremost were clear: bony aquiline visages, jut-nosed, the lips drawn back in strain.

"I count thirteen," said Glystra. "Bishop take four on the left; Corbus four on the right; I'll get five from the middle."

The riders deployed in a near-perfect line in front of the outcrop where the four stood, as if they had lined up to be killed. Three flickers of violet, a crackling of power.

147

Thirteen Rebbirs lay blasted and smouldering on the ground.

A few minutes later they set off across the plain toward the line of cliffs. They rode the four strongest zipangotes; the others had been set free. The Rebbir swords, knives and metal were secure behind their saddles. They wore black cloaks and white helmets.

Nancy found little pleasure in the disguise. "The Rebbirs smell like goats." She made a wry face. "This cloak is abominable. And the helmet is greasy inside."

"Wipe it out," advised Glystra. "If it gets us to Myrtlesee, it's served its purpose . . ."

The land, rising in a long slope, became rocky and barren. The flat-leaved vines and creepers near the lake gave way to stunted thorns of a particularly ugly orange color. The tides of sunlight glared and dazzled, and snow on the Eyrie glittered like white fire.

The region was not without inhabitants. From time to time Glystra, glancing to the side, found white eyes in a pink wizened face staring into his from out of the thorn, and occasionally he saw them running, crouched low, bounding over the rocks.

On the morning of the second day a caravan of six freight-carriers appeared in the distance ahead, sailing swiftly down the wind. From a covert fifty yards off the trail the four travellers watched the caravan whirl past— six swift shapes swinging to the press of white cloth— then they were gone downwind, and soon out of sight toward Lake Pellitante.

On the third day, the escarpment loomed big ahead. The monoline rose in a tremendous swoop, up toward the lip of the cliff.

"That's the way you come down from Myrtlesee," said Glystra. He turned his head, followed the hang of the cable across the sky, up, up, and along, till it disappeared against the chalky front of the cliff. "Going up wouldn't be so easy. That's a long portage. But down . . . Remember the ride down into the Galatudanian Valley?"

Nancy shivered. "This would be worse. . . ."

They came to the landing at the end of the monoline, where the portage must start. The trail led off to the left, slanting up over the basal detritus of crumbled boulders. Then it cut back, into a way dug out of the very side of the cliff and curbed with cemented masonry. Two hundred yards in one direction, then back, traversing— right, left, right, left—and the shoulders of the zipangotes rubbed the inner wall, so that it was necessary to sit with the inside leg looped over the pommel of the saddle. The zipangotes swept up the trail easily, gliding on six legs with no suggestion of effort.

Up, up, back, forth. The face of Big Planet dropped below, spreading wider and wider, and where an Earthly eye might expect a horizon, with a division into land and sky, there was only land, and then still more land. Lake Pellitante glanced and gleamed in the distance. A feeder river came down from the north, circling out of the Eyrie, and stained the earth yellow with its swamps. The outlet river, which they had crossed on rafts, swept broadly south-east, presently breaking into a series of exaggerated meanders, like a crumpled silver ribbon, and then vanished into the south.

Up, up. Wind drove a scud of clouds at the cliff; suddenly the trail was cloaked in damp gray twilight, and the wind swept up the mountain with the sound of a roaring torrent.

The fog glowed yellow, dispersed in trails and wisps; the sun shone full on their backs. Glystra's beast shoved its horny face over the last hump, surged with its four hind feet, and stood on flat ground.

They halted near the edge of the cliff, with the wind pressing up over the rim. The plateau was bare limestone, scoured and free of dust. Gray-white, featureless, it stretched twenty miles flat as a sheet of cardboard; then became mottled, a region of gray shadows. The intervening area was empty except for the monoline: the standards at fifty-foot intervals and the cable dwindling to nothing like an exercise in perspective.

"Well," said Glystra, "nothing in sight, so—"

"Look," said Corbus in a flat voice. He pointed north, along the rim of the cliff.

Glystra slumped back into the saddle. "Rebbirs."

They came along the verge like a column of ants, still several miles distant. Glystra estimated their number at two hundred. In a thick voice he said, "We'd better get moving . . . We can't kill them all. If we ride along the monoline—not too fast—perhaps they won't bother us. . . ."

"Let's go!" said Corbus.

At a careless lope the caravan started east, down the copy-book perspective of the monoline. Glystra kept an anxious watch on the company to the north. "They don't seem to be following—"

"They're coming now," said Corbus.

A dozen of the cavalry spurted forward out of the ranks, raced out at a slant evidently bent on interception.

Glystra clenched his teeth. "We've got to run for it."

He dug his knees into the side of the zipangote. It

moaned and mumbled and flung itself ahead, bony face straining against the wind.

Twenty-four heavy feet pounded back the limestone. And behind came the Rebbirs, black cloaks flapping out behind.

15

The Rebbirs

Nightmare flight, thought Glystra; was he asleep? Nightmare steeds, nightmare riders, the gray-white flat given depth only by the diminishing monoline: a nightmare vista permeated by fear and strangeness and pitilessness. . . .

He broke free of the sensation, cast it away. Turning, he watched the Rebbirs over his shoulder. The whole army had streamed out, as if stimulated by the excitement of the chase. The first dozen had not gained appreciably; Glystra stroked the horny side of his mount with an emotion almost like affection. "Go to it, boy. . . ."

Miles, changeless miles: flat gray plains, thunder of pounding feet. Looking ahead, Glystra saw that they were near the region of mottled shadows—dunes of sand, white as salt, crystalline and bright as broken glass.

The Rebbirs had drawn closer, apparently able to extract the most frantic efforts from their mounts. Ahead—the dunes: sand swept off the flatland and piled in huge rounded domes.

Looking behind, Glystra saw a sight which thrilled him, one which might have been beautiful in other, less personal circumstances. The Rebbirs in the van had risen to their feet, standing in wonderful balance on the backs of their plunging mounts. And each, throwing back his cloak, fitted an arrow to a heavy black bow.

The bows bent; behind the arrows Glystra glimpsed keen faces: eagle cast to nose, forehead, chin. A chilling wonderful sight . . . He yelled, "Duck! They're shooting at us!" And he crouched over the side of his beast.

Thwinggg! The shaft sang over his head. The dunes towered above. Glystra felt the feet of his mount sound with a softer thud, a scuffing, and they were coursing across white sand . . . The creature was laboring, breath was seizing in its throat. Very few miles left in the clogged muscles, then they would be at bay, the four of them. Their ion-shines would kill ten, fifteen, twenty, fifty— then there would be a sudden surge of hawk-faced men, a raising of swords, a chopping. . . .

Over the dunes, down the soft round valleys, up to the milk-white crests. Then looking back to view the surge of black-cloaked riders pouring across the swells, like black surf.

The dunes ended, washed against black obsidian hills. Behind, the rumble of multitudinous feet, hoarse war-calls . . . Out of the dunes, into an old water-course through the flint, where possibly once or twice yearly water foamed. The zipangotes stumbled over chunks of fractured black volcanic glass with sagging necks, bent legs.

To either side gullies draining the side areas opened. Glystra swerved to the left. "In here!" He was panting, in sympathy with the gasps of the zipangotes. "Quick! If we can lose them, we've got a chance. . . ."

He plunged into the gully; behind came Nancy, pale, white around the mouth, then Bishop, then Corbus.

"Quiet," said Glystra. "Back into the shadows—" He held his breath as if he could control the rattling sobs of his beast.

Thudding sounded out in the main watercourse. Black

things hurled past the opening. War-calls sounded now loud, now dim.

There was a sudden slackening to the sounds, an ominous change of pitch. Calls vibrated back and forth—questioning tones, answers. Glystra turned, looking behind. The ravine sloped at a near-impossible angle up to a ridge.

Glystra beckoned to Nancy. "Start up the hill." To Bishop and Corbus: "After her."

Nancy kneed her mount. It moved, mumbled, stopped short at the slope, lowered its skull, tried to turn.

Nancy hauled the reins, kneed the beast desperately. Coughing and whimpering, it set its first pair of feet above its head on the slope, scrambled up.

"Quick!" said Glystra in a harsh whisper. "They'll be here any minute!"

Bishop and Corbus followed . . . The yelling sounded closer. Glystra turned his mount up the slope. Steps sounded behind him, a snuffling. Silence. Then a cry loud and brilliant, the loudest sound Glystra had ever heard. From all directions came answering calls.

Glystra kneed his mount up the slope. Behind came the Rebbir, leaning forward with his sword out-stretched, waving it like an eager antenna.

The gully was choked with hot-eyed men and their horny black beasts. The steep slope was a mass of clawing legs, hulking shoulders.

Nancy breasted over the ridge, then Bishop, then Corbus, then Glystra.

Corbus knew what to do. He laughed, his white teeth shining. His ion-shine was ready. He aimed it at the first Rebbir zipangote, squeezed. The white skull-head shattered into a scarlet crush. The beast threw up its front legs like a praying mantis, poised briefly, swung gradually over backwards, fell into the beasts behind.

A tangle of writhing flesh. White skull-faces, despairing eagle-men, a horrid tangle at the bottom of the slope—a talus of hot jerking flesh, the horny bodies of the zipangotes, the softer sinews of men, clotted together like hiving bees.

Glystra whirled his mount, led the way along the ridge. They rode with all the speed left to their beasts, threading the line of the ridge past the incursions of gullies, ravines, gulches. Caves and blow-holes opened under their feet.

After five minutes Glystra turned down one of the gullies, halted behind a heavy wall of vitreous slag.

"They'll be a long time finding us now, if they even bother to look . . . We'll be safe until dark, at any rate."

He looked down at the heaving shoulders of his mount. "You're not much of a looker—but you've been quite a friend. . . ."

After nightfall they returned to the ridge and stole eastward through the dark. The ridge crumbled into rotten gray rock, disappeared under a dim ocean of sand.

As they started across the flat, from far behind came a call, an eerie hooting which might or might not have been human. Glystra halted his zipangote, looked up toward the Big Planet constellations, listened. Silence everywhere.

The zipangote shuffled its feet, snorted softly. The distant call came once more. Glystra shifted in his saddle, kneed the zipangote into motion. "We'd better put distance between us and the Rebbirs while it's still dark. Or at least until we find concealment of some sort."

They set off quietly across the glimmering sand. Glystra watched over his shoulder. A spatter of meteorites scratched bright lines down the sky. From far back came the mournful call once more.

Big Planet rolled on through space, twisting its shoulder back toward Phaedra. Dawn came, a pink and orange explosion. By this time the zipangotes were barely able to stumble and their heads swung on long necks, sometimes striking the ground.

The light grew stronger. A silhouette, low in the east, appeared—vegetation, waving fronds, bearded stalks, tendrils trailing from splayed branches.

Phaedra burst up into the sky. Plain to be seen now was an island of vegetation ten miles long in a white sea. From the center rose a hemispherical dome, glistening as of pale metal.

"That must be Myrtlesee," said Glystra. "Myrtlesee Fountain."

There was no area of transition. Desert became oasis as sharply as if a knife had trimmed away any extraneous straggles of herbage. Blue moss grew fresh and damp; an inch away the clay lay as dry and arid as any twenty miles to the west.

Passing into the cool gloom was like entering the Garden of Paradise. The air smelled of a hundred floral and leafy essences, damp earth, pungent bark. Glystra slid off his mount, tied the reins to a root, helped Nancy to the ground. Her face was pinched and white, Bishop's long countenance was loose and waxy, Corbus' eyes gleamed like moonstones and his mouth was pulled into a thin pale line.

The zipangotes nosed and snuffled in the moss, lay down, rolled over. Glystra ran to remove the packs before they should be crushed.

156

Nancy lay at full length in the shade, Bishop slumped beside her.

"Hungry?" asked Glystra.

Nancy shook her head. "Just tired. It's so peaceful here. And quiet . . . Listen! Isn't that a bird singing?"

Glystra listened, and said, "It sounds very much like a bird." A shadow crossed his face; he frowned, shook his head. He dismissed the odd idea which had suddenly been inserted in his mind. And yet—hmm. Strange.

Corbus opened the commissary pack, mixed vitamin concentrate with food powder, moistened it, stirred it into a heavy paste, scraped it into Cloyville's cooker, squeezed down the lid, waited an instant, lifted the lid and withdrew a cake of hot pastry. He contemplated it gloomily. "If we ever get back to Earth I'm going to eat for a month. Ice cream, steak, apple pie, swiss cheese on rye with lots of mustard, strawberry shortcake, corned beef and cabbage, fried chicken, spare-ribs—"

"Stop it," groaned Bishop. "I'm sick as it is. . . ."

Glystra lay down on the moss. "Let's hold a council of war."

Corbus asked lazily. "What's the problem?"

Glystra looked up into the blue-green foliage, tracing the white veins of a leaf. "Survival . . . There were eight of us that left Jubilith, not counting Nancy. You, Bishop, me, Pianza, Ketch, Darrot, Cloyville and Vallusser. Nancy makes nine. We've come a thousand miles and there's only four of us left. Ahead of us is first of all more desert, the main part of the Palari. Then mountains, then the lake and the Monchevior River, then God knows what-all."

"Trying to scare us?"

Glystra continued as if he hadn't heard. "When we left

157

Jubilith, I thought the chances pretty good that we'd all make it. Footsore, bedraggled—but alive. I was wrong. We've lost five men. Our weapons are just about done for. I don't know whether I've got a charge left in mine or not. Big Planet is meaner and tougher than we allowed for. The chances are that we'll be killed if we go on. So— now's the time. Anyone who wants to return to Kirstendale on the monoline has my blessing. There's metal enough in those Rebbir swords to make us all rich men. If any of you feel that you'd rather be a live Kirster than a dead Earthman—now's the chance to make up your minds, and no hard feelings."

He waited. No one spoke.

Glystra still looked up into the leaves. "We'll rest here in Myrtlesee a day or so, and then—whoever wants to start east—" He left the sentence hanging in mid-air. His eyelids were heavy. The warm air, the cool shade, the soft moss, fatigue—all induced drowsiness. He aroused himself with a jerk. Bishop was snoring. Nancy was lying on her side. Corbus sat with his back to a tree, eyes half-closed.

Glystra rose to his feet. "Looks like we're planning to sleep," he said to Corbus. "I'll take first look-out. You can have the second, then Bishop, then Nancy. . . ."

Corbus nodded, stretched out full length.

Glystra paced up and down, clenching and unclenching his hands. It was as if his brain were a house and knocking on the door was a boy with a barrowful of thoughts. Somehow he could not find the key to the door.

He walked softly across the moss, looked down at his companions. Bishop snored, Corbus slept like an innocent child, Nancy's hands trembled, quivered as if in a nightmare. He thought: the traders had killed Pianza, the man on watch, why had they stopped? It would have been perfectly safe to kill the entire party, and the traders apparently lacked qualms of any sort. The Earthmen wore valuable clothes, with many metal accessories. The ion-shines alone represented fortune beyond dreams. Why had not the entire party been slaughtered in their sleep? Was it that the traders had been prevented by someone who carried enough authority, perhaps in the shape of an ion-shine, to enforce his decisions?

Glystra kneaded his knuckles in his palms . . . Why? Had his enemy calculated that without trolleys, they might turn back to Kirstendale? If Pianza had been killed while someone stood acquiescently by, one of these three sleeping before him was not only a spy and a saboteur, but a murderer.

Glystra turned away, the ache of grief and uncertainty in his throat. He walked back into the grove. The moss was like a deep rug of marvellous softness. The air was murmurous, restful. Big Planet sunlight trickled through layers of leaves and open spaces, fell around him with the richness of light in a fairy-tale forest. Through the air came a sweet trilling, soft-flute-like. The song of a bird— no, probably an insect or a lizard; there were no birds on Big Planet. And from the direction of the dome he heard the mellow chime of a gong.

There was a soft sound beside him. He jerked around. It was Nancy. He sighed in relief. "You frightened me."

"Claude," she whispered, "let's go back—all of us." She went on breathlessly, "I have no right to talk this way, I'm an uninvited guest . . . But—you'll surely die, I don't want you to die . . . Why can't we live, you and I?

159

If we returned to Kirstendale—we could live out our lives in quiet. . . ."

He shook his head. "Don't tempt me, Nancy. I can't go back. But I think that you should."

She drew away, searched his face with wide blue eyes. "You don't want me any more?"

He laughed wearily. "Of course I do. I need you desperately. But—it's a miracle that we've come this far. Our luck can't hold out forever."

"Of course not!" she cried. "That's why I want you to turn back!" She put her hands on his chest. "Claude, won't you give up?"

"No."

Tears trickled down her cheeks. He stood awkwardly, trying to formulate words of comfort. They stuck in his throat. Finally, for want of anything better, he said, "You'd better rest," aware that the words sounded stiff and formal.

"I'll never rest again."

He looked at her questioningly. But she went to the verge of the oasis, leaned against a tree and stood looking across the white desert.

Glystra turned away, paced up and down the cool blue moss.

An hour passed.

He walked down to look at Nancy. She lay outstretched, head on her arms, asleep. Something in her posture, in the stiff turning-away of the back, intimated to Glystra that never again would their relationship be quite the same.

He went to where Corbus lay asleep, touched his shoulder. Corbus' eyes flicked open instantly.

"Your watch. Call Bishop in an hour."

Corbus yawned, rose to his feet. "Right."

A sound. Hoarse throbbing sound. Glystra was very tired, very comfortable.

A harsh yammering penetrated the world behind his eyelids. It was a distant urgent sound. Danger, he must awake. *He must awake!*

He jumped to his feet, wide awake, clawing at his ionshine.

Corbus lay beside him, asleep.

Bishop was nowhere in sight. Neither was Nancy.

A crackle of harsh voices. A thud. Another thud. Further voices, dying, fading out.

Glystra ran through the foliage, through vines with heart-shaped leaves, through a clump of red feather-bushes with green flowers. He tripped on a body, stopped short, frozen in terror.

The body was headless. Blood still pumped from the stump. The head was nowhere visible. The body belonged to Bishop's head.

Where was that round head with its brain so full of knowledge? Where was Bishop, where had he gone?

He felt a grasp of his arm. "Claude!" He felt a string on his cheek. He looked into Corbus' face.

"They've killed Bishop."

"So I see. Where's Nancy?"

"Where's Nancy? *Where's Nancy?*"

He turned to look, then halted his gaze, turned to look at the ground at his feet.

"Whoever killed Bishop took her with him," said Corbus. "Looks like her tracks, here in the moss—"

Glystra took a deep breath, another. He looked down

161

at the tracks. Sudden energy fired him. He ran off toward the dome. He passed a circle of slim cypresses, branches laden with golden fruit. He came out on a paved walk, leading straight to the great central dome. The whole face of the building was visible as well as the columned arcades to either side. Neither Nancy nor her captors were in sight.

For an instant Glystra stood stock still, then started forward once again. He ran through the gardens, past a long marble bench, a fountain spraying up six jets of clear water, down a walkway paved with diamond-shaped blocks of white and blue-gray stone.

An old man in a gray wool smock looked up from where he knelt with a trowel in flower-bed.

Glystra stopped, demanded harshly, "Where did they go? The men with the girl?"

The old man gazed blankly at him.

Glystra took a short step forward; the old man cringed.

"Where did they go? Answer me, or—"

Corbus came up behind. "He's deaf."

Glystra glared, swung away. A door opened into a wall at the end of the walkway; this was the door Nancy must have been taken through. He ran over, tried it. It was as solid as a section of the stone wall.

He pounded on it, yelling, "Open up! Open! Open!"

Corbus said, "Pounding on that door won't get you much but a knife in your neck."

Glystra stood back, stared at the stone building. The sunlight had lost its tingle, the gardens were drab and dismal. In a bitter voice he said, "There's nowhere on this planet where a man can walk in peace."

Corbus shrugged. "I guess anything goes anywhere—so long as they can get away with it."

Glystra clenched his teeth; the muscles corded around his mouth. "There's power in this gun to kill a lot of them, and by heaven, I'll see the color of their blood!"

Corbus' voice was tinged with impatience. "We'll do better if we go at the matter rationally. First we'd better take care of our beasts before they're stolen."

Glystra glared defiantly up at the stone wall, then turned away. "Very well . . . You're right."

For a moment they stood by the headless body. "Poor old Bishop," said Glystra.

"We probably won't outlive him more than a day," said Corbus in his flat voice.

The zipangotes stood grunting and growling, bumping the white carapace of their heads against the tree-trunks. Wordlessly Glystra and Corbus loaded the packs, handling the pathetic belongings of Bishop and Nancy with heavy fingers.

Corbus stopped in his work. "If I was running this outfit, do you know what we'd do?"

"What?"

"We'd ride out of here due east as fast as we could make it."

Glystra shook his head. "I can't do it, Corbus."

"There's something fishy going on."

"I know it. I've got to make sure what it is. I'm fighting a lost cause now . . . You can still drift back to Kirstendale."

Corbus grunted.

They climbed into the saddles, rode toward the dome.

16

The Search

The air was full of lazy sounds: the far bird-like trill, a hum of small insects, the rustle of warm wind. They passed a clump of gardenia trees; here stood a girl playing with a diabolo. She had a triangle face, big dark eyes; she wore green satin trousers and red slippers. Wordlessly she watched them pass, mouth a little parted, her toy forgotten, and contemplating her shining cleanliness Glystra became warmly aware of his own bristling filth.

They rode out of range of the girl's curious eyes, past a low wall topped with spheres of polished stone overgrown with colored lichen. Behind came the sound of soft singing. The wall merged into the side of the main dome; skirting the building they rode down a neat lane. A ditch with clean water flowed to the left; to the right was a line of small shops. It was a bazaar like hundreds of others Glystra had passed through while travelling among the stars.

Rugs, shawls, quilts hung over rods; fruits and melons lay heaped in neat pyramids; pottery crocks and vessels lay stacked, their glaze misted by a film of dust; baskets hung from ropes. No one heeded them as they rode past on the moaning zipangotes. In the shadows a few heads were turned and Glystra saw the flash of eyes, but there were no voices raised to greet or sell.

One shop, slightly larger than the others, displayed a wooden sword as a guild-mark. Glystra pulled up his mount. "I've got an idea." He slid free a pair of the swords they had taken from the Rebbirs, carried them into the dimness of the shop.

A short fat man leaning against a heavy table looked up. He had a big pale head, black hair shingled with gray, a sharp nose and chin, the face of a Rebbir changed and rendered devious by civilization.

Glystra flung the swords down on the table. "What are these worth to you?"

The fat man looked at them and his face changed. He did not try to conceal his interest. "Where did you get these?" He reached out, gingerly felt the metal. "These are the finest steel . . . None but the South Rebbir hetman carry steel like this."

"I'll part with them cheap," said Glystra.

The armourer looked up with quick light in his eye. "What is your wish? A sack of peraldines? A four-tier helmet, mother-of-pearl perhaps, crowned by a Magic Mountain opal?"

"No," said Glystra. "It's easier than that. An hour ago my woman was taken into the big dome, or temple, whatever you call it. I want her back."

"Two steel swords for a woman?" demanded the merchant incredulously. "Do you joke? I'll furnish you four-teen virgins beautiful as the morning sun for the two swords."

"No," said Glystra. "I want this particular woman."

The merchant absent-mindedly felt of his neck, stared into the shadow of his shop. "In truth, I covet the swords . . . And yet I own but one head." He stroked the shiny metal with a reverent hand. "Still—each of these blades

165

represents a thousand heads—a thousand bits of iron, melted and annealed, cleared of dross, heated and quenched, honed for half a year." He picked up one of the swords. "The Dongmen are unpredictable; at times they seem foolish and old, and then one hears of their craft and cruelty, so that an honest man never knows what to believe. . . ."

Glystra fidgeted. Time was passing; minutes kneaded dull fingers into his mind. Nancy—his mind wavered sidewise into the possibilities. Then a floor of hardness seemed to rise up under his misgivings. Suppose she were bedded, raped; if that were the worst, there was no irreparable harm done. . . . Possibly she might be allowed a respite. One hour, two hours? Perhaps bathed, perfumed, clothed? It all depended upon the fastidiousness of her captor.

He became aware of the merchant's calculation. "Well?"

"Just exactly what do you want of me?"

"I want this woman. She is young and beautiful. I imagine she has been taken to someone's private chamber."

With an expression of surprise at his ignorance, the merchant shook his head. "The priests are celibate. Only the hierarchs allowed themselves the use of women. More likely she has been taken to the pens."

"I know nothing of the temple," said Glystra. "I want the help of someone who does."

The merchant nodded. "I see. You want help. You'll risk your own head then?"

"Yes," said Glystra angrily, "but drop the idea that you won't be risking yours along with me."

"I won't," said the merchant coolly. "But there is one

who will." He pushed with his foot under the counter. A moment later a chunky young man with a face harder and bonier than his father's entered the room. His eyes fell on the swords; he uttered a sharp exclamation, took a step forward, halted, looked at Glystra.

"My son Nymaster," said the merchant. He turned to the young man. "One of the blades is yours. First you must take this man through Nello's crevice into the temple. Wear robes, take an extra robe with you. This man will point out a woman he wants; no doubt she'll be in the pens. You will bribe Koromutin. Promise him a porphyry dagger. Bring the woman back outside."

"Is that the all of it?"

"That's everything."

"Then the blade is mine?"

"The blade is yours."

Nymaster turned, motioned to Glystra with an air of calm execution. "Come."

"One moment," said Glystra. He went to the door. "Corbus."

Corbus slouched into the room, looked around expressionlessly.

Glystra pointed to the two blades. "If I return with Nancy, this man receives the two swords. If neither of us returns—kill him."

The merchant voiced an inarticulate protest. Glystra glared at him, "Do you think I trust you?"

"Trust?" said the merchant with a puzzled expression. "Trust? What word is that?" And he tested it several times more.

Glystra gave Corbus a wolfish grin. "If I don't see you again—good luck. Set yourself up as an emperor somewhere."

167

The merchant conferred earnestly with his son, gesticulating with the palm of one hand. The son wore a subdued expression.

Nymaster beckoned to Glystra; they left the shop, walked around the building, entered an alley between two fences over which fern fronds fell. Nymaster stopped at a little shed. He pressed heavily on one foot, the door swung open. He reached in, tossed a bundle to Glystra. "Wear this."

It was a white gown with a tall peaked hood. Glystra pulled it over his head. "Now this," said Nymaster—a maroon sleeveless smock an inch shorter than the first garment. "And this"—a loose gown of black still shorter, with a second hood.

Nymaster dressed himself similarly. "It's the wear of a Dongman Ordinary—a lay priest. Once inside the temple no one will look at us." He tied a third set of robes into a neat bundle, looked up and down the alley. "This way—quickly."

They ran a hundred feet to a portal in the fence, passed through into a rank garden of fern. The ground was marshy and quivered underfoot. The ferns crackled and snapped in the wind.

Nymaster halted, then stole forward carefully, stopped once more, held out a hand admonishing silence. Looking past him, through a screen of wire vine, Glystra saw a tall spindly man with a gray concave face and a crooked nose standing idly in the sunlight. He carried a quirt in a long gnarled hand, which he slapped idly against his black boots. A little distance away six children of varying ages squatted in a truck garden, grubbing weeds with sharp sticks. Their ankles were knotted together with greasy twine, their only garment was a loose smock of coarse cloth.

Nymaster leaned back, whispered, "To reach the wall we've got to pass Nello; we can't let him see us, he will raise an outcry."

He bent, picked up a clod, flung it hard at the little boy at the end of the line. The boy cried out, then quickly silenced himself, bent furtively to his work.

Nello uncoiled like a lazy python, sauntered yawning across the sunny garden to the quivering boy and raising his whip, carefully and without haste striped the child's buttocks. Once—twice—three times—

Nymaster pulled at Glystra's arms. "Now while he's absorbed in his enjoyment. . . ."

Glystra let himself be pulled across the patch of open space, behind a wall of crumbling stone. Nymaster scurried now at top speed, the skirts of his garment flapping in three-colored flashes.

By a thick cycad with a trunk like the skin of a pineapple he paused, looked in all directions, and finally peered through the fronds at the top of Myrtlesee dome.

"Sometimes a priest stands in the turret watching across the desert. This is when they expect important guests, and wish to ready the oracle." He peered, squinted. "Hah, there he is, scanning the wide world."

Glystra saw the dark shape in a cage atop the dome, standing stiff as a gargoyle.

"No matter," said Nymaster. "He will never notice us; his gaze is out in the air-layers." He climbed the wall, using chinks and crevices in the rock for foot and hand holds. Halfway up he disappeared from view, and Glystra, following him up the wall, came upon a narrow gap invisible from below.

Nymaster's voice came from below. "The wall was built for show, and hollow. There is an avenue within."

Glystra heard a clink, a click and sparks flew through the darkness. A line of hot smoulder pulsed as Nymaster blew, burst into a tongue of flame, from which he lit a torch.

Nymaster strode ahead confidently, a lord in his own realm. They walked a hundred yards, two hundred yards, across damp well-packed clay. Then the wall ended against blank stone. At their feet was a pit into which Nymaster lowered himself.

"Careful," he muttered. "The footholds are only cut into clay. Get a good toe-grip."

Glystra descended eight feet, ducked under the foundations of a heavy wall, crawled up a slanting passage.

"Now," said Nymaster, "we're under the floor of the Main College. Over there"—he pointed—"is the Veridicarium, where the oracle sits."

Footfalls sounded above—hasty yet light, with an odd hesitancy. Nymaster cocked his head. "That's the Sacristy, old Caper. When he was young a malicious slave poisoned her teeth, and when he made demands on her, she bit his thigh. The wound never healed and his leg is no thicker than a wand."

A second mass of rock barred their way. Nymaster said, "This is the oracle's pedestal. Now we must be careful. Hold your head away from the light, say nothing. If we are halted and recognized—"

"What then?"

"It depends on who the villain is, and his rank. The most dangerous are the novices in black fringes, who are

170

over-zealous, and the Hierarchs, with gold baubles on their hoods. The ordinaries are less conscientious."

"What do you plan?"

"This passage leads to the pens where prisoners, slaves and exchanges are pent before processing."

"Processing? Do you mean serving as an oracle?"

Nymaster shook his head. "By no means. The oracle needs the wisdom of four men to guide his thoughts, and for every dissertation of an oracle three men besides himself must be processed. He himself serves as fourth man, for the next oracle."

Glystra, gripped by a sudden impatience, waved his hand. "Let's hurry."

"Now—absolute quiet," warned Nymaster. He led around the rock, up a rude wooden ladder, from which he rolled off on to a shelf. He fixed the torch in a rope socket, and crawled off on his stomach through the darkness. Glystra came after. Overhead a stone floor pressed into his back.

Nymaster stopped and Glystra ran into his feet. Nymaster listened, then jerked forward.

"Follow me, swiftly."

He disappeared. Glystra almost fell into a dim hole. He swung himself down, stood on a stone floor at Nymaster's back. Vile-smelling water gurgled past his feet. Nymaster strode toward the light, a shaft of feeble yellow shining down a flight of steps. He climbed the steps and without hesitation stepped out into the light.

Glystra followed.

The air was hot and reeked with an oily stench that knotted his stomach. From a wide archway came sounds of industry.

Nymaster marched past without pause. Glystra fol-

lowed on his heels. He turned his head, looked into a
bin—into the blank dead eyes of Bishop.

Glystra made a moaning coughing sound, stopped
short. He felt Nymaster's hard arm, heard his petulant
voice.

"What's the trouble?"

"That is the head of my friend."

"Ah." Nymaster was uninterested. "Beyond is the
extraction room where the head is tapped of its
wisdom. . . .It is a precise art, so I am given to understand, and not easily mastered." He looked sardonically
at Glystra. "Well—?"

Glystra pushed himself away from the wall. "Yes. Let's
get it over with."

By a heroic effort he restrained his gorge. Nymaster
impatiently hurried off down the corridor.

Men in robes passed—two, three, four—without paying
them heed. Then Nymaster stopped short. "There, behind
this wall are the pens. Look in through the chinks and
pick out your woman."

Glystra pressed close to the stone wall, peered through
an irregular hole at about eye-level. A dozen men and
women, completely naked, stood in the middle of the
room, or sat limply on stone benches. Their hair had been
shaved, and their pates daubed with paint of either blue,
green or yellow.

"Well—which one is she?" snapped Nymaster. "That
one at the far end?" This was a long-headed creature with
pendant breasts and a yellow wrinkled belly.

"No," said Glystra. "She's not here."

"Ha," muttered Nymaster. "Hm, this poses a problem

172

. . . Very difficult—and I fear past the scope of our agreement."

"Nonsense!" said Glystra in a deadly voice. "The agreement was to find the woman and bring her out, wherever she was . . . So now take me to her, or I'll kill you here and now."

"I don't know where to look for her," explained Nymaster in a patient voice.

"Find out then!"

Nymaster frowned. "I'll ask Koromutin. Wait here—"

"No. I'll come with you."

Nymaster growled under his breath, and turned off down the passage. He thrust his head into a little chamber. The man within was fat and middle-aged. He wore a spotless white tunic and an immaculate collar of ruffled lace. He appeared soft, pompous, petulant, effeminate, capable of irresponsible spite. He was not surprised to see Nymaster and resentful only to the extent that as an important official, his time was valuable.

Nymaster spoke to him in a low voice, which Glystra bent forward to hear. Koromutin's eyes rested on him, probed under his hood.

"—he says she's not in the pen; he won't leave till he finds her. She must own the key to his life; she must be a witch. No woman is worth such effort and expense. But in any event we must have her."

Koromutin frowned judiciously. "This woman evidently must be pent upstairs for personal use. If so—well, how much does your father put forward? Now I mind me of a certain dagger of good Philemon porphyry. . . ."

Nymaster nodded. "It shall be yours."

Koromutin rubbed his hands, bounded to his feet, examined Glystra with a new speculation. "The woman is

173

evidently a rich queen. My dear sir," he bowed, "I salute your loyalty. Allow me to assist your search." He turned, not waiting for Glystra's answer, flounced down the hall.

They climbed a flight of curving stairs. From above came the sound of footsteps descending. Koromutin bowed with vast obsequiousness.

"Bow!" hissed Nymaster. "The Prefect Superior!"

Glystra bowed low. He saw the hem of priestly robes, exceedingly rich. The white was a silky floss; the red, a fur soft as the pelt of a mole; the black, a heavier fur. A peevish voice said, "Where are you, Koromutin? An oraculation will shortly be in progress, and where is the wisdom? You are remiss."

Koromutin spoke resonant apologies. The Prefect Superior returned upstairs. Koromutin trotted back to his cubicle, where he donned a high-collared garment of stiff white brocade embroidered with scarlet spiders and a tall white conical hat with ear flaps and cheek guards which almost hid his face.

"Why the delay?" hissed Glystra.

Nymaster shrugged. "Old Koromutin holds the post of Inculcator, and that is his ceremonial regalia. We will be delayed."

Glystra said fretfully, "We have no time for it; let's get about our business."

Nymaster shook his head. "Not possible. Koromutin is bound to the oraculation. In any event, I wish to witness the rite; never have I watched an oracle at his revelations."

Glystra growled threats but Nymaster could not be moved. "Wait till Koromutin leads us to the woman. She is not in the pens, you saw as much yourself."

Glystra, fuming and disquieted, was forced to be content.

17

The Oracle

Koromutin continued his preparations. From a locked cabinet he brought a jar of a murky yellow fluid, from which he filled a rude hypodermic.

"What's that stuff?" demanded Glystra contemptuously.

"That is wisdom." Koromutin spoke with unctuous complacency. "The head glands of four men go into each charge; the material is concentrated sagacity."

Hormones, pineal fluid, thought Glystra; God only knew what nastiness.

Koromutin replaced the jar of fluid in the cabinet, clamped the hypodermic to the front of his hat like a holy emblem. "Now—to the Veridicarium."

He led Nymaster and Glystra down the corridor, up the stairs, along a wide passage to the central hall under the dome—a large twelve-sided room panelled with mother-of-pearl and swimming with pale gray color. In the center rose a dais of black wood holding a single chair.

There were only two dozen priests in the hall, arranged in a semi-circle, chanting a litany of monosyllabic gibberish unintelligible to Glystra, and, he suspected, equally meaningless to the priests.

"Only a score," muttered Koromutin. "The Lord Voivode will not be pleased. He bases the value of the oracle's wisdom by the number of priests in the hall ... I must wait here, in the alcove." His voice came muffled as if from under the robes. "By custom, I follow the oracle." He glanced around the hall. "You two had best go by the Boreal Wall, lest some stripling novice peer under your hood and raise an outcry."

Nymaster and Glystra took inconspicuous positions against a great carved screen. A moment later an egg-shaped palanquin curtained with peach satin and fringed with blue tassels was borne into the hall. Four black men in red breeches served as porters; two girls followed with a chair of withe and clever pink bladder cushions.

The porters set down the equipage; a red-faced little man hopped out from between the curtains, seated himself in the chair which was hurriedly thrust under him.

He beckoned furiously, to no one in particular, to the world at large. "Haste, haste!" he wheezed. "Life is running out! The light leaves my eyes while I sit here!"

The Prefect Superior approached him, bowed his head with nicely calculated respect. "Perhaps the Lord Voivode would care to refresh himself during the preliminary rites."

"Devil take the preliminaries!" bawled the Voivode. "In any event I note but a niggardly score of priests here to honor my presence; such makeshift preliminaries I can well spare. Let us to the oraculating; this time let him be a stalwart in his prime—a Rebbir, a Bode, a Juillard. No more like that senile Delta-man who died two minutes after the spasms left him."

The prefect bowed. "We will seek to oblige you, Voivode." He looked up at a sound. "The oracle comes."

Two priests entered the room supporting between them a black-haired man in a white smock. He stared back and forth like a trapped animal, digging his heels into the floor.

The Lord Voivode roared in contempt. "Is this the creature who is to advise me? Faugh! He appears unable to do more than empty his bowels in fear!"

The prefect spoke with imperturbable suavity. "Let your misgivings vanish, Lord Voivode. He speaks with the wisdom of four men."

The wretch in the white smock was hoisted to the chair on the dais, where he sat trembling.

The Lord Voivode watched in ill-concealed disgust. "I believe I can tell him more than he can tell me, even with his wisdom quadrupled; all he knows is fear. And once again the precious instants of my life are wasted futilely; where will I find just treatment?"

The prefect shrugged. "The world is wide; perhaps somewhere oracles exist superior to ours here at Myrtlesee Fountain. The Lord Voivode might with advantage put his questions to one of those other omniscients."

The Voivode spluttered, abruptly lapsed into silence.

Now appeared Koromutin, stately and ceremonious in his stiff gown. He climbed the dais, lifted the hypodermic down from his hat, plunged it home in the oracle's neck. The oracle tensed, arched his back like a bow, flung his elbows out, thrust his chin hard into the air. For a moment he sat rigid, then slumped, limp as seaweed into the chair. He put his head into his hand, rubbing his forehead.

There was dead silence in the chamber. The oracle rubbed his forehead.

His foot jerked. His head bobbed. Sounds came from his mouth. He raised his head in bewilderment. His shoulders quivered, his feet jerked again, his nose twitched. A swift babble poured from his mouth, rising in pitch. He yelled, in a hoarse bawling voice. His body quivered, jerked—faster, faster. He was vibrating as if the dais were rocking.

Glystra watched with fascinated eyes. "Is that the wisdom? I find no sense in this screaming."

"Quiet."

The man was in wildest agony. Moisture dripped from his mouth, his face muscles were knotted into ropes, his eyes glared like lamps.

The Lord Voivode leaned forward, smiling and nodding. He turned to the prefect who bent respectfully, put a query inaudible over the yammer of the oracle. The prefect nodded calmly, straightened, teetered back and forth on his heels, hands behind his back.

The oracle sprang to his feet. His back arched, the breath rattled past lips which were pulled back from teeth . . . Then he settled limply into the chair. He sat still, calm and serene, as if agony had purged away all the dross in his soul and left him with a vast meditative coolness.

In the silence the prefect's murmur to the Voivode was clearly distinguishable: "He's now on the settle. You have perhaps five minutes of wisdom before he dies."

The Voivode hitched himself forward. "Oracle, answer well, how long have I to live?"

The oracle smiled wearily. "You ask triviality—and I shall answer. Why not? So—from the position of your body, from your gait, from certain mental considerations, it is evident that you are eaten by an internal canker. Your breath reeks of decay. I judge your life at a year, no more."

The Voivode turned a contorted face to the prefect.

178

"Take him away; he is a liar! I pay good slaves and then he tells me lies. . . ."

The prefect held up a calm hand. "Never come to Myrtlesee Fountain for flattery or bolus, Voivode; you will hear only truth."

The Voivode turned back to the oracle. "How may I extend my life?"

"I have no certain knowledge. A reasonable regimen would include bland foods, abstinence from stimulating narcotics and gland revitalizers, a program of charitable deeds to ease your mind."

The Voivode twisted angrily back to the prefect. "You have gulled me; this creature voids the most odious nonsense. Why does he not reveal the formula?"

"What formula?" inquired the prefect without concern.

"The mixing of the elixir of eternal life!" roared the Voivode. "What else?"

The prefect shrugged. "Ask him yourself."

The Voivode dictated the question. The oracle listened politely.

"There is no such information in my experience, and insufficient data to synthesize such a formula."

In more gentle tones the prefect suggested, "Ask only such information as lies in the realm of the natural. The oracle is no seer, like the Witthorns or the Edelweiss Hags."

The Voivode's face turned a mottled purple. "How may I best secure my son his inheritance?"

"In a state isolated from external influence a ruler can rule from tradition, by force or by the desire and acquiescence of his subjects. The last of these guarantees the most stable reign."

"Go on, go on!" screamed the Voivode. "Time fleets: You will die at any moment?"

"Strange," said the oracle with a weary smile, "when now for the first time I have started to live."

"Speak!" said the prefect sharply.

"Your dynasty started with yourself when you poisoned the previous voivode; there is no tradition of rule. Your son might therefore maintain himself by force. The process is simple. He must kill all who dispute his leadership. These acts will win him new enemies, and he must kill these likewise. If he is able to kill faster than his enemies are able to gather their strength, he will remain in power."

"Impossible! My son is a popinjay. I am surrounded by traitors, preening cock-o'-the-walk underlings who wait the time of my death as the signal to rob and pillage."

"In this case your son must prove himself a ruler so able that no one will desire to be rid of him."

The Voivode's eyes grew dim. His gaze went far away, perhaps to the face of his son.

"To foster this situation, you must institute a change in your own policies. Examine every act of your officials from the viewpoint of the least privileged members of the state, and modify your policies accordingly; then when you die, your son will be floated on a reservoir of good will and loyalty."

The Voivode leaned back in his chair, looked quizzically up at the prefect. "And it is for this that I have paid twenty sound slaves and five ounces of copper?"

The prefect was disturbed. "He has outlined a course of action to guide you. He has answered your questions."

"But," the Voivode protested, "he told me nothing pleasant!"

The prefect looked blandly up along the mother-of-

180

pearl panelling. "At Myrtlesee Fountain you will hear no flattery, no spurious evasions. You hear exactitude and truth."

The Voivode swelled, puffed, blew out his cheeks.

"Very well, another question. The Delta-men have been raiding all Cridgin Valley and stealing cattle. My soldiers flounder in the mud and reeds. How best may I abate this nuisance? What can I do?"

"Plant bush-vine on the Imsidiption Hills."

The Voivode sputtered; the prefect said hastily, "Explain if you please."

"The Delta-folk subsist by preference on clams. For centuries they have cultivated clam beds. You have grazed your pechavies on the Imsidiption slopes so steadily that the vegetation is gone and the rain washes great quantities of silt into River Pannasic. This silt is deposited on the clam beds, the clams die. In hunger the Delta-men raid the cattle of the valley. To abate the nuisance, remove the cause."

"They have been impudent and treacherous; I want revenge."

"You will never achieve your wish," the oracle said.

The Voivode leapt to his feet. He seized a stone jar from his palanquin, threw it viciously at the oracle, struck him on the chest. The prefect held up an outraged hand; the Voivode darted him a look of black malice, flung aside the girls, jumped into the palanquin. The four black porters silently lifted the poles to their shoulders, started for the door.

The oracle had closed his eyes. His mouth drooped. A tic twisted his lips. He began to gasp—great gulping breaths. His fingers clenched, unclenched. Glystra, watching in fascination, started forward, but Nymaster clutched him, drew him back.

"Are you mad? Do you not value your head?"

Koromutin marched past, motioned significantly. "Await me in the corridor."

"Hurry!" said Glystra.

Koromutin gave him a glance of wordless contempt, disappeared down the passage. An endless ten minutes later he returned, wearing his usual white and blue robe. Without a word or glance he turned up the steps glowing with vermilion lacquer, which gave on an arcade circling the dome. Through tall arches Glystra could see across the oasis, past the shimmer of the desert to the black hills, now hazy in the afternoon light.

Koromutin turned up another flight of stairs, and they came out into another corridor circling the dome. This time the openings overlooked the hall below. Koromutin turned into a small office. A man almost his twin sat at a desk. Koromutin waved Nymaster and Glystra back, approached the desk, spoke with great earnestness, and presently received an answer of equal import.

Koromutin beckoned to Nymaster. "This is Gentile, the Steward Ordain. He can help us, if your father will part with a second dagger of workmanship like that I am to receive."

Nymaster grumbled and cursed. "It can be so arranged."

Koromutin nodded and the little man at the desk, as if waiting the signal, arose, stepped out into the hall.

"He has seen the woman in question," said Koromutin in a confidential undertone, "and can take you to her quarters. I leave you in his care. Walk discreetly, for now you tread in high places."

They continued, with Gentile the steward in the lead—along interminable corridors, up another flight of stairs. Glystra heard a sound which caused him to halt in his tracks—a low-pitched steady hum.

Gentile turned impatiently. "Come now, I will show you the woman, then my task is done."

"What causes that sound?" asked Glystra.

"Look through the grating; you will see the source. It is a glass and metal organism that talks in distant voices—a think of potency, but not of our present interest. Come."

Glystra peered through the grating. He saw modern electronic equipment arranged and hooked together in a manner that suggested knowledgeable improvisation. A rough table held a speaker, a microphone, a bank of controls, and behind, the twenty parallel fins which carried the printed circuits, served as condensers, resistances, impedances . . . Glystra stared, the sight opening an entirely new range of possibilities.

"Come, come, come!" barked the steward. "I wish to keep my head on my shoulders, even if you care nothing for yours."

"How much further?" snapped Nymaster. The affair was taking him farther afield than he had bargained for.

"A few steps, no more, then you shall see the woman; but mind you, take care not to make your presence known or else we'll all dangle and our heads will be drained."

"*What!*" barked Glystra savagely. Nymaster gripped his arm, shook his head urgently. "Don't antagonize the old fool," he whispered. "Otherwise we'll never find her."

18

Charley Lysidder

They continued, walking on heavy green carpet along a corridor which constantly curved out of sight ahead. At last Gentile halted at a door of heavy wood. He looked furtively behind, then stooped with the ease of much practice, peered through the crack where the hinges dented the jamb.

He turned, motioned to Glystra, "Come now, look. Assure yourself of her presence—then we must leave. At any moment the High Dain may appear."

Glystra, smiling grimly, looked through the crack.

Nancy. She sat in a cushioned chair, head back, eyes half-closed. She wore loose pajamas of dull green brocade; her hair was bright and clean, she looked as if she had only just finished scrubbing herself. Her face was blank, expressionless; or rather, she wore an expression Glystra could not identify.

With his left hand Glystra felt for the latch of the door. In his right hand he held his ion-shine. The fat steward squawked. "Stand back, stand back! Now we must depart!" He plucked Glystra's sleeve with angry fingers.

Glystra shoved him away. "Nymaster, take care of this fool."

The door was not locked. He flung it open, stood square in the doorway.

Nancy looked up with wide eyes. "Claude. . . ."

She slowly put her feet to the floor, stood up. She did not rush to him in gladness and relief.

"What's the trouble?" he asked quietly. "What's happened to you?"

"Nothing." Her voice was listless. "I'm all right."

"Let's get moving. There's not too much time."

He put an arm around her shoulders, urged her forward. She seemed limp, dazed.

Nymaster held the steward negligently by the nape of the neck. Glystra looked deep into his frightened and outraged countenance. "Back to the radio room." The steward jerked around, trotted whimpering back along the amber-lit corridor.

Downstairs, back along vaguely remembered ways. Glystra held his ion-shine in one hand, Nancy's arm in the other.

A hum, an electric susurration.

Glystra pushed into the room. A thin man in a blue smock looked up. Glystra said, "Stand up, be quiet and you won't get hurt."

The operator slowly rose to his feet, his eyes on Glystra's ion-shine. He knew it for what it was. Glystra said. "You're an Earthman."

"That's right. What of it?"

"You set up this equipment?"

The operator turned a contemptuous glance along the table. "What there is of it . . . Anything wrong with that? What's your argument?"

"Get me Earth Enclave."

"No, sir. I won't do it. I value my life pretty high, mister. If you want Earth Enclave, call it yourself. I can't stop you with that heater on me."

Glystra took a sinister step forward, but the man's face changed not a flicker. "Stand against the wall, next to the steward . . . Nancy!"

"Yes, Claude?"

"Come in here, stand over by the wall, out of the way. Don't move."

She walked slowly to where he had indicated. She was trembling, her eyes roved around the room, up and down the walls.

She licked her lips, started to speak, thought better of it.

Glystra sat down at the table, looked over the equipment. Power from a small pile—a simple short-wave outfit like that owned by a million high school boys on Earth.

He snapped the "On" switch. "What's the Enclave frequency?"

"No idea."

Glystra opened a file index, flipped to E. "Earth Enclave, Official Monitor—Code 181933." The control panel displayed six tuning knobs. Under the first was the symbol "0," under the second "10," under the third, "100," and so by multiples of ten to the sixth. Evidently, thought Glystra, each knob tuned a decimal place of the frequency. He set the sixth knob to "1," the second to "8"—he looked up, listened.

Footsteps sounded along the wall, heavy hard feet, and Nancy wailed, a wordless sound of desperation.

"*Quiet!*" hissed Glystra. He bent to the dials. "1"— "9"—

The door swung open. A heavy black-browed face looked in. Instantly the steward was on his belly. "Holy Dain, it was never my will, none of my doing. . . ."

186

Mercodion looked over his shoulder into the corridor. "Inside. Seize those men."

Glystra bent to the dials. "3"—one more dial to go. Burly men trooped into the room; Nancy staggered out from the wall, her face drawn and bloodless. She stood in the line of fire. "Nancy!" cried Glystra. "*Get back!*" He aimed his ion-shine. She stood between him and the High Dain. "I'm sorry," whispered Glystra huskily. "It's bigger than your life. . . ."

He squeezed the button. Violet light, ghastly on white faces. A sigh. The light flickered, went out. No power.

Three men in black robes rushed him. He fought, wild and savage as any Rebbir. The table tottered, toppled. In spite of the operator's frantic efforts the equipment crashed, jangled to the floor. At this point Nymaster bolted from the room. His feet pounded down the corridor.

Glystra was fighting from the corner, using elbows, fists, knees. The black-robed men beat him to the floor, kicked his head, wrenched his arms up hard behind his back, punishing him.

"Truss him well," said Mercodion. "Take him down to the pen."

They marched him along the corridors, down the stairs, along the arcade overlooking the oasis.

A black speck streaked low across the sky. Glystra uttered a hoarse cry. "There's an air-car! An Earthman!"

He stopped, tried to pull close to the window. "An Earth air-car!"

"An Earth air-car," said Mercodion easily, "but not from Earth. From Grosgarth."

"Grosgarth?" Glystra's mind worked sluggishly. "Only one man in Grosgarth would own an air-car—"

"Exactly."

"Does the Bajarnum know—"

"The Bajarnum knows you're here. Do you think he owns an air-car and no radio?"

He said to the black-robed men, "Take him to the pens, I must greet Charley Lysidder . . . Watch him carefully, he's desperate."

Glystra stood in the middle of the stone floor, naked, damp, miserable. His clothes had been stripped from him, his head was shaved, he had been drenched in an acrid fluid smelling of vinegar.

These were the pens of Myrtlesee Fountain. The air was gruel-thick with latrine reek and slaughter-house odors, seeping in with the steam from the processing rooms. Glystra breathed through his mouth to escape awareness of the stink. Horrible odor—but it was a poor time to be fastidious. He frowned. Strange. A component of the stench was a heavy, pungent, almost sweet, smell which tickled his memory.

He stood quietly, trying to think. Difficult. The stone floor oozed under his bare feet. Four old women crouching beside the wall moaned without pause. A thin red-eyed man vilified a blowsy woman with waist-long blonde hair, which for some reason had not been shaved. She sobbed into her hands, without apparent attention to the curses of the man—guttural throat-catching sobs. Steam and stench poured in from the processing room through chinks and cracks in the stone, likewise bars of yellow light flickering through the steam. With the light and the steam came the sounds of the processing: boiling, pounding, rasping, loud conversation.

Eyes looked in at him, through the hole to the corridor,

blinked, passed on . . . Unreality. Why was he here? He was waiting to have his head boiled. Like Bishop's head. Pianza was lucky; he lay buried beside the yellow reeds of Lake Pellitante. Cloyville was luckier yet. Cloyville wore a grotesque puff of purple lace on his head, and played at being both master and servant.

This was the low ebb. Nearly the low ebb. Much of a man's dignity went with his hair. There was one more notch to slip—from naked humiliation into the anonymous soup of the processing pots. It was almost foreordained, this last notch. It had been a steady progress down a slope toward lesser and lesser life, morale, power . . . A whiff of the pungent sweet odor came from the processing rooms, stronger than ever. It was definitely familiar. Lemon-verbena? Musk? Hair-oil? No. Something clicked in Glystra's mind. *Zygage!* He went to the wall, peered through a chink.

Almost under his face a tray held four neatly arranged heads, with their brain-pans sawed off to display the mottled contents.

Glystra twisted away his gaze. To the right a cauldron bubbled; to the left a bin held acorn-shaped fruits. Zygage, indeed. He watched in fascination. A man, sweating and pallid, in clammy black leather breeches and a blue neckerchief, scooped up a shovel-full of the zygage acorns, sprinkled them into the cauldron.

Zygage! Glystra turned away from the hole, thinking hard. If zygage were a constituent for the oracle-serum, why, then, the brain-extracts? Probably no reason whatever; probably they were added only for their symbolic potency. Of course he could not be sure—but it seemed unlikely that pituitary and pineal soup would cause wild contortions like those he had witnessed in the Veridicar-

189

ium. Much more likely that the zygage was the active ingredient; such would be the parallel with Earth plant-extracts: marijuana, curare, opium, pejote, a dozen others less familiar.

He thought of his own experience with zygage: exhilaration, then hangover. The oracle's reaction was the same, on a vastly exaggerated scale. Glystra pondered the episode. A miserable terrified wretch had undergone torment and catharsis to achieve a magnificent calm and rationality.

It had been an amazing transformation, baring the optimum personality apparently latent in every human being. How did the drug act? Glystra's mind veered around the question: a problem for the scientists. It seemed to achieve the results of the great de-aberration institutes on Earth, possibly by the same essential methods: a churning through the events of a lifetime, the rejection of all subconscious obsessions and irrationality. A pity, thought Glystra, that a man only achieves this supreme state to die. It was like the hang-over after his smoke-breathing . . . In his brain there was a sudden silence, as if a mental clock had stopped ticking. Bishop had felt no hangover. Bishop had—he recalled Bishop's intensified well-being after the zygage inhalation; apparently his habit of ingesting vitamins had warded off the hangover.

Vitamins . . . Perhaps the oracle died from exaggerated vitamin depletion. And the idea gave Glystra much to think about. He walked slowly back and forth across the damp stone floor.

The woman with the yellow hair watched him dully; the red-eyed man spat.

"*Ssst.*"

Glystra looked toward the wall. Hostile eyes gleamed through the hole. He crossed the room, peered out into the corridor.

It was Nymaster. His tough round face wore an expression of angry discomfort. "Now you lie in the pen," he said in a low urgent voice. "So now you die. What then for my father? Your man will take away the swords, and possibly kill my father, for so you ordered."

True, thought Glystra. Nymaster had served him faithfully. "Bring me paper," he said. "I will write to Corbus."

Nymaster handed through a greasy scrap of paper, a bit of sharp graphite.

Glystra hesitated. "Have you heard anything of—"

"Koromutin says you will be oracle. For Charley Lysidder himself. So the prefect told him while he was beating Koromutin."

Glystra pondered. "Can you bribe me free? I have other metal, other swords like yours."

Nymaster shook his head. "A ton of iron would effect nothing now. Tonight Mercodion has ordained that you burn up your mind for the Bajarnum."

The words sank into Glystra's mind. He stared at Nymaster scratching his cheek with a ruminative finger. "Can you bring Corbus back with you? For another sword of fine steel?"

"Aye," said Nymaster grudgingly. "I can do so . . . A mortal risk—but I can do so."

"Then take him this note, and bring him back with you."

Now the sounds and the stenches of the pen had no meaning for him. He paced up and down, whistling thinly through his teeth.

191

Up, down, up, down, looking across the room at each turn, watching for Corbus' face.

A chilly thought struck him. He had guessed something of the mechanics of the plot against him. After Morwatz had failed, after he had eluded the second expedition by crossing the river Oust and dropping the high-line, he had been left to go his own way to Myrtlesee, but all the time, all the weary miles from Swamp City, he had merely been taking himself to a prearranged trap. The strategy was clear. He had been left to execute it himself. Suppose Corbus was part of the machinery? At this moment nothing was unthinkable.

"Glystra."

He looked up, turned to the hole. It was Corbus in priest's robes. Glystra glanced right and left, crossed the room.

Corbus looked in at him quizzically. "How goes it?"

Glystra pressed close to the hole. "Did you bring it?" he asked in a whisper.

Corbus passed a little package through the hole. "And now what?"

Glystra smiled thinly. "I don't know. If I were you I'd start back down the monoline to Kirstendale. You can't do any more here."

Corbus said, "You haven't told me what you plan to do with the vitamins."

"I plan to eat them."

Corbus eyed him questioningly. "They been giving you bum chow?"

"No. Just an idea I've got."

Corbus glanced up and down the corridor. "With a big hammer I might make a hole in this wall—"

"No. There'd be a hundred priests out here at the first

click. You go back to the sword-maker's, wait till tomorrow. If I'm not there then I'm never coming."

Corbus said coolly, "There's one or two charges in the ion-shine. I've been half-hoping"—his eyes glistened—"to meet someone we know."

Glystra's throat constricted. "I can't believe it," he muttered.

Corbus said nothing.

"She never had Bishop killed, I'm sure of it . . . It was an accident. Or he tried to stop her."

"No matter how you look at it—she's part of the picture. Four good men killed—Bishop, Pianza, Darrot, Ketch. I'm not counting Vallusser; that little rat was in up to his neck. I've been watching her a long time—ever since she insisted on joining our little suicide club."

Glystra laughed shortly. "I thought all the time it was—that she—" he had no words to finish.

Corbus nodded. "I know. One thing I'll say for her, she put her life on the line alongside ours. She came out on top. She's up there"—he jerked his thumb—"and you're down here. What a stinking hole. What are they cooking?"

"Brains," said Glystra indifferently. "They distil out some kind of nerve juice which they mix with zygage and feed the oracles. It works on the oracles like the smoke worked on the Beaujolain soldiers, only a thousand times more."

"And it kills them?"

"Dead as a mackerel."

"Tonight you're the oracle."

Glystra held up the package Corbus had brought him. "I've got this. I don't know what's going to happen. From here out I'm playing strictly by ear. And," he added, "I may be wrong, but I have a hunch there'll be a few

193

unforeseen developments here at Myrtlesee Fountain and I'm not worrying."

Nymaster appeared behind Corbus. "Come, there's a prefect on his way down. Come quick."

Glystra pressed close to the hole. "So long, Corbus."

Corbus waved his hand non-committally.

19

Wisdom for Lysidder

The sun dropped behind the fronds of Myrtlesee Fountain. A mesh of cirrus clouds flared golden in the sky. Dusk drifted in from eastern lands where night had already fallen over peoples and cities and tribes and castles still unseen.

A marble pavilion extended to the east of Myrtlesee Dome, enclosed by a colonnade of ornate design. Behind the colonnade was a pond of still water, dimly reflecting the afterglow with the fronds and ferns of the grove silhouetted in reverse. Four blond and slender youths bearing torches came from the dome. Their hair was cut in effeminate bangs. They wore skin-tight costumes sewed of red and green diamonds, black satin slippers with curled toes. They set the torches in tripods of dark wood, returned within.

A moment later six men in black kilts carried forth a square table which they placed in the exact center of the pavilion. The blond boys brought chairs, and the men in black kilts marched away in a single file.

The boys spread the table with a gold and brown-striped cloth, giggling like girls. At the center they arranged a miniature landscape—Myrtlesee Fountain in exact detail, complete with dome and pavilion, even to a table on the pavilion, where five persons sat to the light of tiny candles.

Flagons of liquor and wine were bedded in ice, trays of crystallized fruits, tablets of insect gland-wax, cakes of pressed flower petals were laid exactly in place, then the boys went to pose under the flaming torches, consciously beautiful.

Minutes passed. The boys fidgeted. Dusk gave way to feather-soft Big Planet night. Stars gleamed. A syrup-smooth breeze drifted through the colonnade to flutter the torches.

Voices sounded from the dome. Out on the pavilion came Mercodion, the High Dain of Myrtlesee Fountain and Charley Lysidder, Bajarnum of Beaujolais. Mercodion wore his richest robes, with a stole woven of pearls and metal. The Bajarnum wore a gray jacket of heavy soft cloth, red breeches, soft gray boots.

Behind came the Prefect Superior and two nobles of the Beaujolais empire.

Charley Lysidder remarked with pleasure at the table, glanced appreciatively at the statue-like youths, seated himself.

Wine was poured, food was served. Charley Lysidder was in high spirits and Mercodion extended himself to laugh graciously at his jovialities. Whenever there was silence a girl blew chords on a flute. When one of the diners spoke, she stopped instantly.

Ices and sorbets were brought in glass goblets, and finally pots of fuming incense were placed before each of the diners.

"Now," said the Bajarnum, "now for our oracle, Claude Glystra. Originally I had planned to question him under torture, but the oraculation will prove easier for all concerned. He is a man of wide experience and knowledge; he will have much to impart."

"A pity that such brief opportunity exists to plumb his wisdom."

The Barjarnum shook a finger. "It is a matter you must concern yourself with, Mercodion—the maintenance of longer life in your oracles."

The High Dain bowed his head. "It is as you say . . . And now I will order the oracle prepared and we will go to the auditorium."

The hall was crowded with the rustling black-gowned priests. By custom hoods were not worn at night, but the characteristic motivation of reducing individuality to the lowest common denominator was expressed by a white head cloth banded loosely around the forehead, around the nape of the neck, forward under the chin.

Special ceremonial chants had been ordained. Twelve choirs situated each to a wall, mingled their voices in a twelve-part polyphony.

The Barjarnum, Mercodion and their retinue entered the hall, strolled to benches before the oracle's dais. A serious-faced girl with shining blonde hair appeared at a side door. She wore black silk pantaloons and a gray-green blouse. For a moment she paused in the doorway, then slowly crossed the room, the only woman among hundreds of men, a peacock among crows. Eyes covertly followed her, tongues moistened celibate lips.

She stopped beside the Barjarnum, looked down at him with an oddly searching expression. Mercodion bowed politely. The Barjarnum smiled a cold tremble-lipped smile. "Sit down."

The expression of intentness vanished, her face became blank. She sat quietly beside the Barjarnum. A whisper, a buzz, a rustle of garments rose from the spectators. By rumor the woman was the new toy of the High Dain. Eyes curiously probed his face, but the sallow skin was set like the rind of a pudding and no emotion appeared.

A sad chime sounded; a second tremor ran through the hall, a shifting of stance, a motion of eyes. The Bajarnum suddenly seemed to become aware of the assemblage; he muttered to the High Dain, who nodded, rose to his feet.

"Clear the hall. All must go."

Murmuring, dissatisfied, the priests filed out the great doors. The hall was now near-empty, and reverberated with echoes of every movement.

A second chime sounded; the oracle appeared. Two prefects stood by his side, the Inculcator in his stiff white gown and tall hat followed close to the rear.

The oracle was wrapped in a robe of gray and red, and white swathing veiled his head. He walked slowly, but without hesitation. At the dais he paused and was lifted to the oracle's seat.

The silence in the hall was like the inside of an ice-cave. Not a breath, not a sigh, not a whisper could be heard.

The prefects held the oracle's arm, the Inculcator stepped close behind. He took the hypodermic from his hat, he swung his arm.

The High Dain frowned, squinted, jumped to his feet. "Stop!" His voice was harsh.

The watchers sighed.

"Yes, Dain?"

"Remove the head-swathing; the Bajarnum would look on the man's face."

The prefect hesitated, then reached forward, slowly unhitched the white burnoose.

The oracle looked straight ahead, down into the eyes of the Bajarnum. He smiled grimly. "If it isn't my old shipmate, Arthur Hidders, dealer in leather."

198

The Bajarnum made a slight inclination of the head. "More people know me as Charley Lysidder." He examined Glystra with a narrow scrutiny. "You appear nervous, Mr Glystra."

Glystra laughed, rather shakily. Enormous overdoses of vitamins, amino and nucleic acids were reacting on his motor system like stimulants. "You do me an honor of which I hardly feel myself worthy——"

"We shall see, we shall see," said the Bajarnum all too easily.

Glystra's eyes went to Nancy. She met his eyes a moment, then looked away. He frowned. Seen in the new context beside the man he had known as Arthur Hidders, she took on a new identity—one not unfamiliar. "The nun," he exclaimed.

Charley Lysidder nodded. "Rather a clever disguise, don't you think?"

"Clever—but why was it necessary?"

The Bajarnum shrugged. "A fur-and-leather-dealer might conceivably accumulate enough Earth exchange to make the old world pilgrimage—but hardly likely that he would bring his talented young concubine with him."

"She's talented all right."

Charley Lysidder turned his head, examined Nancy with dispassionate appreciation. "A pity, really, that she had to become a base tool of policy, she is apt at finer things . . . But that fool Abbigens dropped the ship too far from Grosgarth and I had no one at hand to serve me. Yes, a pity, since I will never use a woman fresh from another man's couch. And now she must find another patron." He glanced humorously at Mercodion. "I fancy that she will not need to seek far, eh, Dain?"

Mercodion flushed, darted an angry glance at Lysidder.

199

"My tastes are perhaps as nice, in some respects, as yours, Bajarnum."

Charley Lysidder settled back in his seat. "It's no matter; I have uses for her in Grosgarth. Let us proceed with the oraculation."

Mercodion waved his hand. "Continue."

The Inculcator stepped forward, raised the hypodermic.

The point stung deep into Glystra's neck. There was a feeling of injection, of pressure.

The prefect's grip tightened on his arms, tensing in anticipation of his motion. He noticed that Nancy had turned her face to the floor; the Bajarnum of Beaujolais, however, watched the proceedings with lively interest.

A great dark hand clamped on his brain. His body expanded enormously; his arms felt twenty feet long; his feet were at the bottom of a cliff; his eyes were like two long pipes leading out on the world. The Bajarnum's voice came like a sibilant whisper in a vast cave.

"Ah, now he squirms. Now it takes on him."

The prefects held Glystra with practiced ease.

"Look!" exclaimed the Bajarnum delightedly. "Look how he flails about . . . Ah, he has caused me much trouble, that one. Now he pays the price."

But Glystra felt no pain. He had passed beyond mere sensation. He was reliving his life, from earliest foetus up through the years, reliving, re-experiencing, re-knowing every detail of his existence. Reviewing these events was a great super-consciousness, like an inspector watching a belt of fruit. As each distorted concept, misunderstanding, fallacy appeared, the hand of the inspector reached down, twitched events into rational perspectives, smoothed out the neural snarls which had clogged Glystra's brain.

Childhood flickered past the super-awareness, then early life on Earth, his training among the planets of the System. Big Planet bulked outside the space-ship port, again he crashed on the Great Slope of Jubilith; again he set out on the long journey to the east. He retraced his route through Tsalombar Woods, Nomadland, past Edelweiss, the River Oust, Swamp Island, down the monoline through the Hibernian March, Kirstendale, across the desert toward Myrtlesee Fountain. Present time loomed ahead; he plunged through like a train coming out of a tunnel. He was once more aware and conscious, with the whole of his life rearranged, all his knowledge ordered into compartments, ready for instant use.

The High Dain's voice came to his ears. "You see him with his brain purged and clear. Now you must hasten; in a few minutes his life-force dwindles and he dies."

Glystra opened his eyes. His body was at once warm and cool, tingling with sensitivity. He felt strong as a leopard, agile, flooded with potential.

He looked around the hall, studied the troubled faces of the people before him. Victims they were, the result of their inner warps. Nancy was pale as eggshell, her eyes full and moist. He saw her as she was, divined her motives.

The Bajarnum said doubtfully, "He looks perfectly happy."

Mercodion answered, "That's the common response. For a brief period they float on a sea of well-being. Then their vitality fails and they go. Hurry, Bajarnum; hurry if you wish knowledge."

Charley Lysidder spoke in a loud voice. "How can I

buy weapons from the System Arms Control? Who can I bribe?"

Glystra looked down at the Bajarnum, at Mercodion, at Nancy. The situation seemed suddenly one of vast humor; he found it hard to control his face.

The Bajarnum repeated the question, more urgently.

"Try Alan Marklow," said Glystra, as if imparting a precious secret.

The Bajarnum leaned forward, excited in spite of himself. "Alan Marklow? The chairman of the Control?" He sat back, a pink flush, half-anger, half-anticipation, on his face. "So Alan Marklow can be bought—the sanctimonious scoundrel."

"To the same extent as any other member of the Control," said Glystra. "That is the reasoning behind my advice: if you plan to bribe any of them, the best person to subvert is the man at the top."

The Bajarnum stared. The High Dain's eyes narrowed. He jerked upright in his seat.

Glystra said, "As I understand it, you want weapons so that you may extend your empire; am I right?"

"In essence," the Bajarnum admitted warily.

"What is the motive behind this desire?"

Mercodion raised his head, started to bellow an order, thought better of it, clamped his mouth in a tight white line.

The Bajarnum reflected. "I wish to add glory to my name, to make Grosgarth the queen city of the world, to punish my enemies."

"Ridiculous. Futile."

Charley Lysidder was nonplussed. He turned to Mercodion. "Is this a usual manifestation?"

"By no means," snapped Mercodion. He could contain

his fury no longer. He leapt to his feet, black brows bristling. "Answer the questions directly! What kind of oracle are you, evading and arguing and asserting the ego which you must know has been numbed by the drug of wisdom? I command you, act with greater pliability, for you will die in two minutes and the Bajarnum has much he wants to learn."

"Perhaps my question was inexact," said the Bajarnum mildly. He returned to Glystra. "What is the most practical method for me to acquire metal weapons at a low cost?"

"Join the Star Patrol," said Glystra waggishly. "They'll issue you a sheath-knife and an ion-shine free."

Mercodion exhaled a deep breath. The Bajarnum frowned. The interview was not going at all as he had expected. He tried a third time. "Is it likely that Earth-Central will forcibly federate Big Planet?"

"Highly unlikely," said Glystra, with complete honesty. He thought it was almost time to die, and sank limply into the chair.

"Most unsatisfactory," grumbled Mercodion.

Charley Lysidder chewed his lip, surveyed Glystra with his deceptively candid eyes. Nancy stared numbly; for all his sharpened perceptions, Glystra could not fathom her thoughts.

"One more question," said the Bajarnum. "How can I best prolong my life?"

Only by the sternest measures could Glystra control his features. He responded in a weak and doleful voice, "Allow the Inculcator to shoot you full of wisdom-stuff, as he has me."

"Faugh!" spat Mercodion. "The creature is insufferable! Were he not three-quarters dead, I swear I would run him through . . . Indeed—"

But Glystra had slumped to the dais.

"Drag the hulk to the 'toir-room," roared Mercodion. He turned to Charley Lysidder. "A miserable mistake, Bajarnum, and if you wish, a second oracle will be prepared."

"No," said the Bajarnum, thoughtfully surveying Glystra's body. "I wonder only what was his meaning."

"Aberrated mish-mash," scoffed Mercodion.

They watched the prefects take the body from the hall.

"Strange," said Charley Lysidder. "He seemed completely vital—a man very far from death . . . I wonder what he meant . . . "

A naked man stole through the night, trailing the odor of death. He came through Nello's garden plot, ducked into the alley, quietly approached the street.

No one was in sight or ear-shot. He trotted quietly through the shadows to the house of the sword-smiths.

Light glowed yellow through the shutters. He knocked.

Nymaster opened the door. He stood stock-still, his eyes bulging. A second man came to look suspiciously over his shoulder—Corbus, who stared a breathless moment. "Claude," he said huskily, "You're—you're—" his voice broke.

Glystra said briskly, "We've got to hurry. First a bath."

Corbus nodded wryly. "You need something of the sort." He turned to Nymaster. "Fill a tub. Get some clothes."

Nymaster turned away wordlessly.

"They hauled me to their abbatoir," said Glystra. "They threw me in a bin full of corpses. When the head-boiler came with his knife, I jumped out at him, and he went into a fit. I escaped through the wall."

"Did they pump you full of nerve-juice?"

Glystra nodded. "It's quite an experience." During his bath he gave Corbus and Nymaster an account of his adventures.

"And now what?" Corbus asked.

"Now," said Glystra, "we do Charley Lysidder one in the eye."

Half an hour later, slipping through the gardens, they looked out on the marble courtyard where the Bajarnum's air-boat rested. A man in a scarlet tunic and black boots lounged against the hood. An ion-shine at his waist.

"What do you think?" whispered Glystra.

"If we can get in it, I can fly it," said Corbus.

"Good. I'll run around behind him. You attract his attention." He disappeared.

Corbus waited two minutes, then stepped out into the court-yard, levelled his ion-shine. "Don't move," he said.

The guard straightened, blinked angrily. "What's the—" Glystra appeared behind him. There was a dull sound; the guard sagged. Glystra took his weapon, waved to Corbus. "Let's go."

Myrtlesee Fountain dwindled below them. Glystra laughed exultantly. "We're free, Corbus—we've done it."

Corbus looked out across the vast dark expanse. "I won't believe it until I see Earth Enclave below us."

Glystra looked at him in surprise. "Earth Enclave?"

Corbus said tartly. "Do you propose to fly to Grosgarth?"

"No. But think. We're in a beautiful position. Charley Lysidder is marooned at Myrtlesee Fountain—without his air-car, without his radio to call for another, if he owns one."

"There's always the monoline," said Corbus. "That's fast enough. He can be back in Grosgarth in four days."

"The monoline—exactly. He'll use the monoline. That's where we'll have him."

"Maybe easier said than done. He won't venture out unless he goes armed to the teeth."

"I don't doubt it. He might conceivably send someone else back to Grosgarth, but only if he owns another air-car. We'll have to make sure. There's a spot, as I recall, where the monoline passes under a bluff, which should suit us very well."

Corbus shrugged. "I don't like to play a string of luck too far—"

"We don't need luck now. We're not the poor hag-ridden fugitives that we were; we know what we're doing. Before the Bajarnum was hunting us; now we're hunting him. Right down there—" Glystra pointed "—that bald-headed bluff. We'll settle on top and wait out the night. Early tomorrow—if he's coming at all—we should see Charley Lysidder scudding west under full press of sail. He'll want to get back to Grosgarth as soon as possible."

20

Vacancy in Beaujolais

Some two hours after dawn a white speck of sail came drifting across the desert from the green smudge that was Myrtlesee Fountain.

"Here comes the Bajarnum," said Glystra, with evident satisfaction.

The trolley drew closer, swinging and swaying with the changing force of the wind. It was a long pack-car, equipped with two long lateen booms, and flew down the line gracefully as a white swan.

With a hum and spin of great wheels the contrivance of wood and canvas slid under them, whirled on into the west. Four men and one woman rode the platform: Charley Lysidder, three Beaujolain nobles in scarlet tunics, elaborate black felt hats and black boots—and Nancy.

Glystra looked after the diminishing sail-car. "None of them wore pleasant expressions."

"But they all wore ion-shines," Corbus pointed out. "It'll be a risky business going near them."

"I don't intend to go near them." Glystra rose to his feet, started back toward the air-car.

Corbus said with mild testiness, "I don't mind chasing after you if I know what you've got on your mind; but if you ask me you're carrying this superman business a little too far."

Glystra stopped short. "Do I really give that impression?" He looked reflectively across the sandy wastes toward the green paradise of Myrtlesee. "Perhaps it's the normal state of the psyche after such a traumatic shock."

"What's the normal state?"

"Introversion. Egocentricity." He sighed. "I'll try to adjust myself."

"Maybe I'll take a dose of that poison too."

"I've been thinking along the same lines. But now— let's catch Charley Lysidder." He slid into the air-car.

They flew west, over the tortured hills of obsidian, the mounds of white sand, the rock flat, over the verge of the great cliff. They slanted down, skimmed low over the tumble of rock and scrub, already shimmering in the morning heat.

The monoline rising to the lip of the cliff etched a vast flat curve, a spiderweb line against the sky. Glystra veered west, flew a mile past the bottom platform, landed under one of the stanchions. "Here we violate the first of Clodleberg's commandments: we cut the line. In fact we excise a hundred feet—the length between two of the stanchions should be enough."

He climbed one pole, slashed the line; Corbus did the same at the second.

"Now," said Glystra, "we double the line, tie the bight to the under-frame."

"Here's a swingle-bar; that suit you?"

"Fine. Two round turns and a couple half-hitches should do the trick—" he watched while Corbus made the line fast. "—and now we go back to the bottom anchor."

They returned to the platform from which the monoline rose to the lip of the cliff. Glystra landed the air-car in the

208

shadow of the platform, jumped to the landing. "Pass up one of those ends from under the boat."

Corbus pulled one of the trailing lengths clear, tossed it up.

"Now," said Glystra, "we make fast to the monoline with a couple of rolling hitches."

"Ah," said Corbus. "I begin to catch on. The Bajarnum won't like it."

"The Bajarnum is not being consulted . . . You get into the car, in case the weight of the monoline starts to drag . . . Ready?"

"Ready."

Glystra cut the monoline at a point four feet past the first of his hitches. The line sang apart, the connection to the air-car took hold, and a long wave swerved up the line and out of sight. The air-car now served as the bottom anchor to the monoline.

Glystra joined Corbus. "I give them about an hour. A little less if the wind is good."

Time passed. Phaedra shouldered huge and dazzling into the dark blue Big Planet sky. Off into the brush a few albino savages lurked and peered. Insects like eels with a dozen dragonfly wings slid easily into the air, threading the harsh gray branches. Round pink toads with eyes on antennae hopped among the rocks. At the top of the cliff appeared a spot of white.

"Here they come," said Corbus.

Glystra nodded. "The ride of their life coming up."

The white spot at the top of the cliff dipped over the edge, started down the long curve. Glystra chuckled. "I'd like to watch the Bajarnum's face."

He pushed down the power-arm. The car lifted from

behind the platform, climbed into the air—up, up, as high as the lip of the cliff. The trolley rolled down into the lowest section of the loop, slowed, hung suspended, helpless. Five black dots were the passengers—agitated, outraged, uncertain.

Glystra flew above the trolley to the monoline landing at the top of the cliff, settled on the platform. The second length of line under the air-car he made fast to that section of the monoline which led over the cliff. He cut it, and now the trolley with its five occupants hung entirely suspended from the air car.

Glystra peered over the brink. "There he is, the Bajarnum of Beaujolais, trapped fair and square, and not a hand laid on him."

"They've still got their guns," said Corbus. "No matter where we set 'em down, they still can shoot at us—even if we take them as far as the Enclave."

"I've considered that. Dousing them in a lake will cool Charley Lysidder's temper as well as short out his ionshines."

The Bajarnum's face, as he stood dripping on the sand beach, was pinched and white. His eyes glinted like puddles of hot quicksilver; he looked neither left nor right. His three noble companions somehow contrived to maintain their dignity even while water sucked squashily in their boots. Nancy's hair clung dankly to her cheeks. Her face was blank as a marble mask. She sat shivering, teeth chattering audibly.

Glystra tossed her his cloak. Draping it over her shoulders and turning away, she slipped out of her sodden garments.

Glystra stood holding the ion-shine. "Now one at a time into the car. Corbus will search you for knives and hooks

210

and like unpleasantness on the way." He nodded to the Bajarnum. "You first."

One by one they passed Corbus, who extracted three daggers, the sodden ion-shines, and a deadly little poison slap-sack from the group.

"Back in the car, gentlemen," said Glystra, "as far back as possible."

The Bajarnum said in a voice soft as the hiss of silk, "There shall be requiting, if I must live two hundred years to see it."

Glystra laughed. "Now you spit nonsense, like an angry cat. Any requiting to be done will be for the hundred thousand children you've sold into space."

The Bajarnum blinked. "There has been no such number."

"Well—no matter. A hundred or a hundred thousand—the crime is the same."

Glystra climbed up into the seat beside Corbus, sat looking down into the five faces. Charley Lysidder's emotions were clear enough: serpent-spite and fury behind the mask of the small features in the too-big head. The three noblemen were uniformly glum and apprehensive. And Nancy? Her face was rapt, her thoughts were clearly far away. But Glystra saw neither fear, anger, nor doubt. Her brow was clear, the line of her mouth was natural, almost happy; her eyes flickered with the passage of her thoughts like the flash of silver fish in dark water.

Here, thought Glystra in sudden insight, is the conflict of multiple personalities resolved; she has been at war with herself; she has been caught in a flow too strong to resist; she submits with relief. She feels guilt; she knows she will be punished; she awaits punishment with joy.

211

They were all settled. He turned to Corbus. "Let's go. Think you can find the Enclave?"

"Hope so." He rapped his knuckles on a black cabinet. "We can find our way along the radio-beam after we get around the planet."

"Good."

The air-car rose into the air, flew west. The lake vanished astern.

Charley Lysidder wrung water from the hem of his cloak. He had recovered something of his suavity and spoke in a thoughtful voice. "I think you wrong me, Claude Glystra. So indeed I have sold starving waifs, but as a means to an end. Admittedly the means was uncomfortable, but did not people die before Earth became federated?"

"Then your ambition is to federate Big Planet?"

"Exactly."

"To what purpose?"

The Bajarnum stared. "Why—would not there then be peace and order?"

"No, of course not—as you must know very well. Big Planet could never be unified by conquest—certainly not by the Beaujolain army mounted on zipangotes, and not in your lifetime. I doubt if you care for peace and order. You have used your army to invade and occupy Wale and Glaythree, both quiet farm-countries, but the gypsies and the Rebbirs roam, ravage, murder at will."

Nancy turned, eyed the Bajarnum dubiously. The three nobles glared truculently. Charley Lysidder preened a ring in his mustache.

"No," said Glystra, "your conquests are motivated by

212

vanity and egotism. You are merely Heinzelman the Hell-horse in better-looking clothes."

"Talk, talk, talk," sneered Charley Lysidder. "Earth commissions come and go, Big Planet swallows them all; they drown like gnats in Batzimarjian Ocean."

Glystra grinned. "This commission is different—what there's left of it. I insisted on complete power before I took the job. I do not recommend; I command."

The Bajarnum's tight features squeezed even closer together, as if he were tasting something bitter. "Assuming all this were true—what would you do?"

Glystra shrugged. "I don't know. I have ideas, but no program. One thing is certain: the slaughter, the slaving, the cannibalism must stop."

"Hah!" The Bajarnum laughed spitefully. "So you'll call down Earth warboats, kill the gypsies, the rebbirs, the nomads, the steppe-men, all the wandering tribes across Big Planet—you'll build an Earth Empire where I would build a Beaujolain Realm."

"No," said Glystra. "Clearly you do not grasp the crux of the problem. Unity can never be imposed on the peoples of Big Planet, any more than a state could be formed from a population of ants, cats, fish, monkeys, elephants. A thousand years may pass before Big Planet knows a single government. An Earth-dominated Big Planet would be unwieldly, expensive, arbitrary—almost as bad as a Beaujolain Empire."

"Then what do you plan?"

Glystra shrugged. "Regional organization, small regional guard-corps . . ."

The Bajarnum sniffed. "The whole decrepit paraphernalia of Earth. In five years your regional commanders become petty tyrants, your regional judges are soliciting

213

bribes, your regional policy-makers are enforcing uniformity on the disparate communities."

"That indeed," said Glystra, "is where we must tread warily. . . ."

He looked out the window across the sun-drenched Big Planet landscape. An endless vista, forested mountains, green valleys, winding rivers, hot plains.

He heard a muffled nervous cry. He twisted to find two of the men in red tunics on their feet, crouching to leap. He twitched the ion-shine; the men in the damp red tunics sank back.

Charley Lysidder hissed a word Glystra could not hear; Nancy shrank to the side of the boat.

There was ten minutes of acrid silence. Finally the Bajarnum said in a crackling self-conscious voice, "And, may I ask, what you plan with us?"

Glystra looked out the window again. "I'll tell you in another couple of hours."

They flew across an island-dappled sea, a gray desert, a range of mountains with white peaks reaching angrily up into dark blue sky. Over a pleasant rolling country dotted with vineyards, Glystra said to Corbus, "This is far enough, I think. We'll set down here."

The air-boat touched ground.

Charley Lysidder hung back, his delicate features working. "What are you going to do?"

"Nothing. I'm turning you loose. You're on your own. You can try to get back to Grosgarth if you like. I doubt if you'll make it. If you stay here, you'll probably have to work for a living—the worst punishment I could devise."

Charley Lysidder, the three noblemen, sullenly stepped out into the afternoon sunlight. Nancy hung back. Lysidder gestured angrily. "I have much to say to you."

214

Nancy looked desperately at Glystra. "Won't you let me out elsewhere. . . ."

Glystra shut the door. "Take 'er up, Corbus." He turned to Nancy. "I'm not setting you down anywhere," he said shortly.

Charley Lysidder and his three companions became minute shapes, mannikins in rich-colored clothes; rigid, motionless, they watched the air-car swing across the sky. Charley Lysidder raised his fist, shook it in a frenzy of hate. Glystra turned away, grinning. "Now there's no more Bajarnum of Beaujolais. Vacancy, Corbus; need a job?"

"I believe I'd make a medium-to-good king . . . Come to think of it," Corbus ruminated, "I've always wanted a nice little feudal domain in a good wine country . . . Fancy uniforms, operettas, beautiful women . . ." his voice trailed off. "Anyway, put my name down for the job."

"It's yours, if I've anything to say about it—and I have."

"Thanks. My first official act will be to clean out that den of fakers, Myrtlesee Fountain. Or does my empire run that far?"

"If you want Myrtlesee Fountain you've got to take the Palari Desert and the Rebbirs along with it."

"Draw the boundary along the River Oust," said Corbus. "I know when I'm well off."

Big Planet landscape, swimming in the halcyon light of late afternoon, slipped astern. Glystra finally found it impossible to ignore the quiet figure in the rear of the car. He stepped down from the control platform, settled upon the seat beside her. "As far as I'm concerned," he said

215

gruffly, "I'm willing to believe that you were an unwilling accessory, and I'll see that—"

She interrupted him in a low and passionate voice. "I'll never be able to make you believe that we were working for the same things."

Glystra grinned a wry sad smile, remembering the journey east out of Jubilith. Darrot, Ketch, Pianza, Bishop: all dead, and if not by her direct action, at least with her connivance. An angel with bloody hands. In order to win his confidence she had feigned love, prostituted herself.

"I know what you're thinking," she said, "but let me speak—and then you may drop me anywhere, in the middle of the ocean if you like.

"The gypsies burnt my home with all inside," she added in a dull voice. "I told you so; it is true. I wandered to Grosgarth, Charley Lysidder saw me at the Midsummer Festival. He was crying crusade against all the outside world, and here, so I thought, was how Big Planet might be made safe and evil beings like the gypsies exterminated. He called me to his chambers; I did not refuse. What girl refuses an emperor? He took me to Earth; on the way back we learned of your plans. Apparently you projected nothing more than the persecution of Charley Lysidder. I was bitter against Earth and all its people. They lived in wealth and security, while on Big Planet the great-grandchildren of Earth were murdered and tormented. Why could they not help us?"

Glystra started to speak; she made a weary gesture. "I know what you will say: 'Earth can only wield authority over a finite volume of space. Anyone who passes through the boundaries forfeits the protection of those within.' That might have been valid for the first ones to come out

216

from Earth, but it seems cruel to punish the children of these thoughtless ones forever and ever . . . And it seemed that while you would do nothing to help us, you wanted to thwart the only man on Big Planet with vision and power: Charley Lysidder. And much as it hurt me, because—" she darted him a brief look—"I had come to love you, I had to fight you."

"Why didn't you?" asked Glystra.

She shuddered. "I couldn't. And I've lived in misery . . . I can't understand how you failed to suspect me."

"When I think back," said Glystra, his eyes on the past, "it seems as if I knew all the time, but could not make myself believe it. There were a hundred indications. Morwatz' troopers had us bound and helpless; you refused to cut us loose until it was clear that the Beaujolains were dead and the gypsies were coming. You thought the Fountain insects sounded like birds. There are no birds on Big Planet. And when Bishop was killed—"

"I had nothing to do with that. I tried to slip off to the dome. He came after me and the priests killed him and took his head."

"And Pianza?"

She shook her head. "The traders had already killed Pianza. I kept them from killing everyone else. But I let them take the trolleys, because I thought that if you would only return to Kirstendale we could live together safe and happy . . ." She looked at him and her mouth drooped. "You don't believe anything of what I'm saying."

"No, on the contrary, I believe everything . . . I wish I had your courage."

Corbus' voice came raucously down from the control platform. "You two are beginning to embarrass me. Clinch and get it over with."

217

Glystra and Nancy sat in silence. After a moment Glystra said, "There's a lot of unfinished business behind us . . . On our way back we'll drop in at Kirstendale and hire Cloyville to pull us around the streets in a big carriage."

"Count me in," said Corbus. "I'll bring a long whip."